BPO DIARY

MOHIT GHANSELA

Made with ♥ on the Notion Press Platform
www.notionpress.com

Contents

Preface

First, a big thanks to my manager—truly an inspiration. He's the kind of guy who acts like he knows how the Big Bang started or how to solve world hunger, while we, the team, just sit back and wonder if he's making it up as he goes. He's been in this company for 12 years—twelve!

Twelve! That's either a testament to his unmatched loyalty or a glaring sign that no other company dared to recruit him.

I sometimes wonder—did he even pass the interview, or did HR just see him wearing a tie and think, "He looks responsible enough—let's give him the job!"

To my colleagues, who somehow manage to survive the daily circus, thanks for sticking it out. And to the readers about to dive into the chaotic world of BPO—welcome to the madness!

Enjoy the ride, and remember: if you ever feel stuck, just think of my manager. If he can make it 12 years here, you can make it anywhere!

Acknowledgements

"I'd like to express my gratitude to all the BPO agents out there who have unknowingly inspired this book with their dedication, humor, and resilience. Your tireless effort behind the screen is something most people will never truly understand.

And of course, to the customers—without you, we wouldn't have jobs. Even if your chats sometimes make us question our life choices, we appreciate your patience."

Prologue

Welcome to the BPO Life

Before we dive in, let me quickly apologize to anyone whose feelings might get hurt while reading these chapter. After all, as they say, the truth is sometimes bitter. But don't worry, I promise to keep it light and funny—after all, working in a BPO is like being in a comedy show, only you're the punchline half the time.

Let's get to the good stuff: the world of BPO—Business Process Outsourcing. It sounds all high-tech and professional, right? In reality, it's where you get paid to handle a tornado of chaos with a smile, solving problems you didn't even know existed. Whether it's picking up calls, answering chats, replying to endless emails, or even managing social media complaints, it's like being a juggler in a circus, except the balls are questions, angry customers, and the occasional tech glitch.

So, here's the deal: you've probably imagined a glamorous job where you're lounging in your pajamas, sipping coffee, and working from the comfort of your home. But soon enough, you realize it's a daily grind—answering calls, handling live chats, and pretending to understand a customer's issue when you've literally Googled it five seconds before they start speaking. This, my friend, is the magical land of BPO, where every customer is a riddle wrapped in a mystery, and every chat feels like you're trying to solve it while juggling flaming torches.

But let's be honest: you didn't choose the BPO life. The BPO life chose you. Or maybe it was the only job that didn't immediately reject your resume with a "Thank you, but no thank you" response.

Now, what exactly is BPO? Let me break it down for you in the simplest terms:

•Business: A customer has a problem.

•Process: You, my friend, are the solution to that problem, equipped with nothing but a headset (or, let's be real, your fingers if you're chatting) and a script that you've learned 30 seconds before the call.

Outsourcing: You're doing all of this for a company located halfway across the world, and you might never meet the person you're helping. Yet somehow, you're expected to solve their problems as if you were their personal tech guru.

ONE

TICKET TO THE BPO CIRCUS

This story begins at a point in life most of us are painfully familiar with—the post-graduation job hunt. Ah, graduation! That magical moment when your college hands you a piece of paper they like to call a degree and, in the same breath, silently whispers, "Good luck out there, kid." No placements, no roadmap—just a mountain of useless assignments and the vague hope that somehow, you'll figure out how to adult.

Spoiler alert: you don't.

Now, I'm not saying all colleges are like this, but let's be real—most are. One day, you're drowning in projects, last-minute submissions, and exams that test nothing but your ability to memorize. The next, you're tossed into the real world with nothing but a flimsy piece of paper and a LinkedIn profile that screams "Please hire me."

So, with a shiny new degree in one hand and my self-esteem clinging on for dear life in the other, I set out to carve a career for myself. Destination? Gurgaon.

Why Gurgaon, you ask? Well, my ever-optimistic friend—let's call him Mr. Overconfidence—swore on everything holy that he could "guarantee" me a job. Now, guarantee is a funny word. In my naive little brain, it meant "a secure, well-paying job handed to me on a silver platter." In reality, it meant "I'll casually mention your name to someone and hope they don't ignore me."

Before I could even think about jobs, interviews, or Gurgaon, I had to survive something far more intimidating—home.

Staying at home post-graduation is like being trapped in a never-ending loop of grocery runs, unsolicited advice, and expertly crafted guilt trips. Every morning, I woke up to a fresh lecture, wrapped delicately in concern and seasoned with just the right amount of sarcasm. And if I dared to complain, I was swiftly reminded of "how expensive everything has become these days."

Especially tomatoes.

Tomatoes had somehow become the new currency of financial distress. Every conversation about the economy circled back to their ever-rising price, as if my joblessness was directly responsible for their inflation.

Somewhere between these guilt-tripped lectures and unexpected tomato economics, I had a realization—I had unknowingly become my family's biggest investment.

From the moment I was born, my existence had been a long-term financial plan. My parents had bet everything on me, expecting that one day, I'd land a good job and turn into their personal human fixed deposit—one that would start delivering high-interest returns after graduation. And now, as they patiently waited for their investment to mature, the reminders were constant.

"When are you going to start earning?"

"By the way, can you also buy potatoes while you're out?"

So, in an act of pure survival, I made the executive decision to leave.

But leaving wasn't as simple as dramatically packing my bags and walking out like a movie hero. No, it required something far more powerful—money. Specifically, money for a train ticket to Gurgaon. And in an Indian household, asking for money isn't a simple transaction—it's a courtroom drama.

The moment I brought it up, the interrogation began:

"Why Gurgaon?" (Because clearly, working for free at home is my

best career option!)
"What if you don't find a job there?" (As if jobs are stray dogs just waiting to adopt me.)
"Why can't you look for a job here?" (Of course, because our local market is overflowing with high-paying opportunities for fresh graduates with zero experience.)

Indian parents have a unique talent for mixing love and sarcasm so masterfully that you end up feeling like a selfish traitor for simply trying to build a future. But after a few rounds of emotional blackmail, countless guilt-tripping glances, and one final, heartfelt "Don't forget to call us when you reach," I was handed the money.

Booking the ticket felt like winning a battle against the very forces of parental love.

With my ticket in hand, I packed my bag, bid farewell to the endless nagging, the bottomless tiffin boxes, and, of course, the eternal tomato inflation crisis.

It was time to step into the unknown.

As I boarded the train, a strange cocktail of emotions swirled inside me—relief, nervousness, and maybe a pinch of excitement. The train was more than just a mode of transport; it was a vessel carrying me toward the unknown, a fresh start.

The journey to Gurgaon felt like the first step in rewriting my future. No more endless chores and guilt trips at home. No more lectures about tomato inflation. This was my grand attempt to turn my shiny new degree into something valuable—something that would finally make my parents believe they hadn't wasted all those years of tuition fees and late-night study sessions on me.

I leaned back in my seat, staring out the window at the blur of passing scenery. I had heard those inspiring rags-to-riches stories—the ones where people left home with nothing but ₹500 in their pockets and somehow built empires worth crores. And here I was, clutching a whole ₹7,000. Forget empire-building—at this rate, I could probably buy the entire universe and still have enough left over for a chai and samosa.

In my mind, I was already negotiating with the USA, reminding them of their promise to back the dollar with gold. “You can’t break this promise,” I’d say, “because I’ve got a universe to run here!” Oh, the world would kneel at my feet. I was the new ruler of the universe, pulling the strings of international policies, fixing global issues like some all-knowing guru.

It was all so magnificent—until the train screeched to a halt, snapping me out of my daydream.

Gurgaon Station.

My heart did a nervous somersault. This was it. The beginning of my journey. The first step in this grand, unpredictable adventure.

The train doors creaked open, and I stepped onto the platform, momentarily disoriented by the chaos around me. The station was alive with a thousand people, each lost in their own little world, yet all bound together by the same frantic energy. I adjusted my bag, which somehow felt heavier now, even though I had packed only the essentials—clothes, a few toiletries, and my dreams.

I glanced around, searching for a sense of direction. Gurgaon. The place where my ambitions—no matter how exaggerated—were supposed to come alive. The platform was nothing like the cozy, familiar world I had left behind. The noise, the rush, the constant motion—it was like stepping into an entirely different universe. And here I was, just another tiny speck in the grand scheme of things, trying to find my place.

Taking a deep breath, I straightened my back and stepped forward. There was no turning back now. The journey had just begun.

I pulled out my phone and called my friend. He gave me an address, told me to grab an auto-rickshaw, and hung up with a casual, “See you soon, bro.”

Full of confidence, I waved down an auto-rickshaw and showed the driver the address. He gave me a quick once-over, as if assessing both my financial status and my survival skills, then nodded.

"200 rupees," he said.

"200 rupees?" I gasped, as if he had just asked for my kidney. "Bhaiya, I think you've misunderstood. This place is in Gurgaon, not on the moon!"

But the driver remained unfazed, probably having heard every bargaining excuse known to mankind.

I tried a different approach. "If I give you 200 rupees, how will I manage to confront the USA about their gold-dollar problem? You're messing up my entire financial strategy here!"

The driver sighed, unimpressed with my global ambitions. "Sir, either pay 200 or step aside. I've got other passengers waiting."

And that's how Gurgaon welcomed me—with a reality check, courtesy of an auto-rickshaw driver.

After some expert-level haggling (a skill every middle-class Indian learns from birth), I managed to bring him down to ₹150. Feeling victorious, I hopped into the auto and officially began my journey into Gurgaon.

As we navigated the bustling streets, something caught my eye. A man on a bike was giving someone a ride—but the pillion rider was paying him for it. Wait. Was that... a paid bike lift?

Back home, giving someone a ride was either an act of kindness or a friendship obligation. Here? Even favors had price tags. Maybe this was why people like me had to leave our small towns for bigger cities—because here, everything was a business.

Anyway, I thought to myself, "Once I solve this whole gold-dollar situation, I'll sort this out too."

As we got closer to my destination, I noticed something else—the streets kept getting narrower, while the buildings grew taller.

It was like a perfect metaphor for Gurgaon itself—cramped spaces, but towering ambitions.

Finally, after what felt like 30-40 confusing turns, countless moments of "Bhaiya, yeh kaunsa rasta hai?" and multiple near-death experiences involving Gurgaon's infamous traffic, the auto driver pulled over and announced,

"Bas, yahi hai. U Block."

I stared at him, then at the street, then back at him. U Block?

And then it clicked—maybe it's called U Block because the roads twist and turn so much, like the letter 'U.' Or maybe Gurgaon just enjoys making people question their navigation skills. Either way, I had survived.

I paid the driver, stepped out, and looked around. That's when I saw him—, my dear friend, standing there, waiting for me.

His expression? "I told you this would be easy" and "Welcome to Gurgaon, my friend."

Before I could even take a proper breath of this so-called "new beginning," my eyes locked onto something that made me freeze in my tracks.

Right there, in the middle of the street, stood a boy and a girl—casually smoking together.

Now, this wasn't just any casual smoking session. No, no. This was history in the making.

For a moment, my brain short-circuited. Oh my god. Equality is finally here!

It was a beautiful sight. A true cinematic moment. Gender norms? Shattered. Societal expectations? Burning away with every drag of that cigarette. It was as if the universe had orchestrated this scene just to remind me that the world was changing, and I, a mere observer, had just witnessed a revolution in progress.

But before I could fully absorb my newfound enlightenment, something even more shocking demanded my attention.

The road—or what I had foolishly assumed was a road—was covered in a suspicious amount of water.

Now, if there's one thing that brings out my inner child, it's puddles. Instinct kicked in, and before I knew it, I was hopping around like a kid who'd just spotted his first monsoon rain.

"Baarish hui thi kya?!" I asked my friend, my voice full of genuine excitement.

His response? A dramatic eye-roll so intense that I genuinely feared for the stability of his eyeballs.

"Could you please not do these things?" he said, exasperated. "This is not rainwater. This is gutter water."

I froze—mid-jump, my foot still hovering above the murky abyss.

And just like that, my romanticized "Bollywood rain moment" transformed into a horror movie plot twist.

Oh, Gurgaon. Where even the puddles come with a backstory and an existential crisis.

When I arrived, my friend wasn't alone. He was with another guy, whom he casually introduced as his roommate.

As soon as I laid eyes on them and took in the situation I was stepping into, a thought crossed my mind: This story could have ended right here.

I could've turned around, grabbed the remaining money from my pocket, booked a return ticket, and gone back to my hometown, where life was simpler, more predictable, and I wouldn't have to face the looming pressure of becoming the family asset.

But, no. Life had bigger lessons in store for me. I couldn't just back out now. After all, that money I borrowed from my parents wasn't just cash—it was an investment—and my parents expected a return. And that responsibility? It was following me like a shadow, always there, quietly reminding me that my next move had better count.

As we walked toward their "room," I took in the surroundings. Something felt... off.

"Wait a second," I said, stopping in my tracks. "Do you call this a flat?"

My friend gave me a smirk, like he was in on a joke I wasn't.

"Yeah, it's a flat. Why?" he asked, clearly confused by my hesitation.

"Because before we do anything else," I said, gesturing dramatically, "you should feed this flat a good meal and fatten it up first! This isn't a flat—it's the size of a matchbox!"

The room was so tiny that I could practically touch both walls just by standing in the middle. The cramped space made me realize something—the real reason I was here wasn't for company or to help me "settle in." No, they needed me to contribute to the rent, because even the two of them combined couldn't afford it.

That's when it hit me. This wasn't just a new city—it was the beginning of my real adventure in Gurgaon. And somehow, I'd already stepped into a role I hadn't fully signed up for: the temporary third roommate with an unspoken financial obligation.

I'm not saying that Gurgaon's ridiculously high flat rents should be regulated—that's not really my job, after all. I'm not about to start an activism movement for affordable housing.

But you know what? Ministers these days are bold enough to tell middle-class people that the stock market isn't meant for them. So, who's to say? Maybe tomorrow they'll make another announcement, like, "These flats and rooms aren't for you small-town folks either."

Anyway, it's not my place to deep dive into such matters. I have bigger things to focus on—like fixing the gold and dollar issue, of course!

So, the "room rules" were simple: only two people could officially stay there, but the rent? Oh, that was conveniently split among the three of us.

And when the landlord showed up for his "inspections"? Well, that's when I had to put on my best tourist act—smiling, nodding, and pretending I was just visiting from out of town.

Oh my god, I realized—I was probably the first person in history paying money to become an illegal migrant in my own country, and all with a perfectly legitimate Aadhaar card!

So, the whole reason I had come to Gurgaon in the first place—getting a job—finally hit me. And, well, it hit me hard, mostly because my precious, hard-earned (okay, borrowed) money was disappearing faster than a magician's trick.

One minute, I was rolling into the city with dreams as big as the skyscrapers around me, feeling like the world was my oyster. The next, I was checking my wallet like it was the last chocolate in the fridge—only to find it was already gone. Poof! Like some magic trick I didn't even ask for.

Now, you might be wondering, How did the money vanish so quickly? Well, let's just say "miscellaneous" expenses played a huge role in this disappearance. The food, the water, the little things you need to survive in a city like Gurgaon—all seemed to have their price. Breakfast? Paid. Lunch? Paid. Dinner? Of course, paid. Every meal felt like a small transaction, adding up with each passing day.

And here's the kicker—you might be surprised to know that most people living in rented houses in Gurgaon, just like me, eat only once at home and once at the office to save money.

Add to that the random little things I had to buy—like a new charger because, apparently, my old one had "mysteriously" stopped working—and before I knew it, the money was just gone.

It was like I was paying for the bare essentials, yet it felt like the essentials were eating up everything, leaving me with nothing but an empty wallet and a lot of regret.

At this point, I decided to pause my ambitious plans of solving the gold-dollar issue and focus on something more achievable: using my parents' money—and their dreams of my education—wisely. After all, I was the asset of the family, not a liability.

My friend, ever the helpful one, handed me the number of a consultancy, promising they'd land me a job in Gurgaon. The catch? To get a job in Gurgaon, I first had to go to Delhi. Yep, you read that right. The irony of this wasn't lost on me for a second—"Need a job in Gurgaon? Sure, just take a detour to Delhi first!" It was like saying, "Want to go to the moon? First, take a pit stop on Mars."

But hey, who was I to argue? I had dreams, a near-empty wallet, and absolutely no plan B. So, with all the enthusiasm of someone about to attend a mandatory family gathering, I packed my wallet (which might as well have been a purse at this point) and set off for Delhi, determined to make things work. Because when life hands you ridiculous logistics, you just have to roll with it, right?

So, with all my hopes pinned on this consultancy and a wallet so light it could've floated away, I finally made it to their office. When I walked in, my heart almost stopped, like someone had hit the pause button on my life.

My hands were trembling so much that I looked like I was auditioning for a role in a thriller movie—the kind where the lead character has a nervous breakdown while signing their life away. And my forehead? Let's just say it was as if I'd just run a marathon under the blazing sun, crossed the finish line, and then forgotten to drink any water. I could practically feel the sweat dripping down in slow motion, like a dramatic soap opera moment where the camera zooms in on your face for maximum intensity.

But hey, no pressure. It's just my entire future hanging in the balance.

The place itself was... well, let's say it was just slightly bigger than my flat, which wasn't saying much. If my flat was the size of a matchbox, this office was more like a slightly larger matchbox—still cramped, but with a few more people to make it feel like a full-blown party. And speaking of people, the place was packed to the brim with candidates.

I mean, I honestly started wondering if they were handing out free iPhones or, better yet, free jobs. There were so many people that it felt like someone had posted a sign saying, "Free entry into Gurgaon—just bring your dreams and a resume!" The competition was real, and the air was thick with hope—and, let's be honest, possibly the scent of a hundred nervous colognes, all battling for attention.

And then there were the consultants. These 4-5 people sitting behind a table, juggling the dreams of what felt like half of India. They were the real unsung heroes, like the Avengers of the job market, only with fewer capes and a lot more laptops. As I sat there, I couldn't help but think, "These guys should run for elections. Look at them—handling this chaos with the patience of saints, listening to every single person's story, and still somehow managing to give everyone that little glimmer of hope in their eyes. What a service to the nation!" I mean, if they could manage this, they could definitely manage an entire country. Maybe they could teach the government how to deal with chaos—without the colognes.

Among the consultants was a woman named Tripti, who finally called me over. I was practically bouncing in my seat, ready to tackle whatever came my way. She asked for my documents, and in my overenthusiastic "first step to success" mode, I handed her every single piece of paper she requested—even the ones she probably didn't need, like my school certificate from class 8 and the receipt for my last haircut. Better safe than sorry, right?

Then came the moment that almost gave me a mental breakdown: "Call or chat?"

I froze. Call or chat? What was this, some sort of tech-savvy game show? My mind was racing, trying to figure out if I'd missed a memo about a new career challenge. I blinked at her, completely confused, until she clarified, "Are you comfortable with handling calls or chats?" Oh, right. It wasn't a trick question. It was just a gentle reminder that I was a fresher—a term that basically screamed, "Hey, you're a rookie, welcome to the job market, where experience is everything, and you have none."

Naturally, I responded, "Whatever is good for me." I was just hoping for the chance to get my foot in the door, whatever it took. After a quick check of my vocabulary (because, let's be real, I had no idea how to use words like "synergy" without looking it up first), she said, "For you, chat would be best."

Well, that was a first. I'd always thought I was good at talking, but apparently, typing was where my real skills lay. Maybe this was the universe's way of telling me I was more of a keyboard warrior than a phone-call hero. At least I wouldn't have to stumble through awkward pauses during calls.

And let me tell you something about being a fresher: it's basically career death. Everyone wants experience, but no one's willing to give you a chance to get it. It's like being stuck in a loop of rejection, where every door you try to open just slams in your face. But these consultants? They were different. Sure, they were going to pay me peanuts, but they were actually offering me options—a chance to start somewhere.

Compared to my college, where placements were more of a myth than a reality, these guys were practically saints. At least they weren't pretending to be saviors while quietly failing to deliver.

For the first time in my life, I had a wild thought—Maybe this consultancy is actually better than my entire college placement cell. I mean, let's be honest: my college's placement department was like that one uncle who keeps promising to help you find a job but never actually does anything beyond forwarding "motivational" WhatsApp messages.

But here? This was different. This place was alive with energy, like a well-oiled job-distributing machine. People were actually getting hired! And for the unlucky ones who weren't? The consultants looked so heartbroken, you'd think they had just watched the saddest Bollywood climax ever.

Any minute now, I expected one of them to wipe their tears and say, "Humne bahut koshish ki, par hum kisi ko job nahi dila paaye..." (We tried so hard, but we couldn't get them a job...)

I was in awe. These people deserved national recognition. Forget Filmfare Awards and cricket trophies—give these consultants the President's Medal! Right after the army, of course. After all, they were fighting a different kind of war—one against unemployment, and let's be honest, against the terrible resumes freshers bring in.

Just as I was soaking in this newfound admiration, a voice jolted me back to reality:

"Come on, it's your turn. Sit down and look at the camera. You don't have to do anything; we'll guide you step by step."

Ah yes, just what every fresher needs to hear before their first corporate interrogation.

This was the first round, which they very dramatically called the "aptitude test." Honestly, calling it a test was giving it way too much respect. I didn't even have to break a sweat—everything was being handled by the consultants themselves. It felt like one of those school exams where you accidentally sit next to the class topper and just happen to copy all the answers. The only difference? Here, it was completely legal.

And the best part? Not a single annoying fly buzzing around, no invigilators pacing the room like they were guarding state secrets—just me, a screen, and a consultant clicking away like a pro hacker. I could've taken a nap, and the result would've been the same.

Before I could even process what was happening, boom—first round cleared! Should I have been ecstatic? Probably. But somehow, the consultants were way more excited than me. Their energy was off the charts, like I had just won an Olympic gold medal in staring at a computer screen.

And then came the inevitable moment: "Now, wait for the second round." Ah yes, the classic let's-make-you-sit-here-forever move.

For the second round, they handed me a list of questions. The very first one was, "Do you know what BPO is?"

And that's when it hit me—I was actually applying for a BPO job! Oh. My. God.

I swear, BPO is such a cute little word. It sounds so fancy, so corporate, like something straight out of a LinkedIn success story. "Hey, I work in a BPO." See? It just rolls off the tongue so smoothly, like butter on a hot paratha.

For a moment, I felt like I was living in a Honey Singh song—

"BPO mein kaam tu karti
Ishaara Pehne hai
Saturday ko party sharty,
Tere bhi kya kehne hai!"

Bro, it was destiny! My career and my rap song aesthetic were aligning like planets before a solar eclipse. I had already started picturing my weekends—work hard on weekdays, party on Saturdays, and sleep till noon on Sundays. Life was looking sorted!

I leaned in slightly, trying to sound as casual as possible, and asked, "Do I have to pay anything?"

But in my head, I was already rehearsing my "Sorry, brother, I don't have any money" speech, complete with the right amount of helpless expression and tragic backstory. I had it all planned—the slight head tilt, the sigh, maybe even a dramatic pause for effect.

Just as I was about to deliver this masterpiece of financial despair, the consultant casually said, "Don't worry, the hiring company pays us. You don't have to spend a single rupee."

Oh.

Well, that was anticlimactic. Here I was, all set for an emotional monologue, and they didn't even give me a chance to use it. I felt like an actor who had memorized all their lines, only for the director to cut the scene last minute.

So that's how they made their money. I had been mentally preparing for an intense bargaining session, ready to argue like a seasoned Delhi street shopper, but it turned out there was no scam—just a legit process. Honestly, I felt a little cheated—not because they were charging me, but because I didn't get to deliver my well-rehearsed "I don't have money" speech.

The second round kicked off, and I was more than ready. I had memorized my introduction like a student preparing for the final viva, repeating it so many times in my head that I could have delivered it in my sleep.

Question after question, I responded exactly as rehearsed, like a well-oiled machine. Judging by the approving nods and occasional smiles from the panel, it felt like they had already decided to hire me before I even finished speaking.

Then came the moment of truth. One of them leaned forward and asked, "Are you comfortable with this job?"

Without a second of hesitation, I blurted out, "YES!" with so much enthusiasm that even I was caught off guard. It wasn't just a response—it was an emotional outburst, a desperate handshake with destiny.

And just like that, it was over. They told me I was selected, my documents would arrive via email, and my joining date would be confirmed soon. But the real shocker? The job was completely free—no hidden charges, no sketchy payments, nothing.

With all the happiness bubbling up inside me, I felt like the protagonist of one of those feel-good Bollywood movies. You know, the ones where everything goes perfectly for the hero, and you're just waiting for the grand musical number.

I was walking back to my matchbox room, thinking, maybe, just maybe, today is the day my life's grand finale begins. My thoughts were as happy as a kid in a candy store, except I was walking into a rented room that didn't have a single piece of candy.

I called home to share the good news. The moment I told them I'd landed a job, they practically threw a celebration. No one even bothered to ask the critical question—"How much is the salary?" Well, even if they had, what was I going to say? "Oh, it's perfect, the company will pay me just enough to cover my cab fare and keep me fed on instant noodles!" In reality, whatever little money they gave me for expenses, the office was generously matching. I was officially "independent," or at least, that's what I liked to tell myself.

But before I could fully bask in the glory of my "new life," my friend—the eternal interrogator—jumped in with his endless barrage of questions: "Which process are you in? Inbound or outbound? Voice or chat?"

Look, let me tell you something. When you're in an interview, you're a yes-man. Yes, I can work night shifts. Yes, weekends are no problem! You agree to everything because the goal is simple: Get the job. But the moment that job is yours? Oh, that's when the real you starts showing up. It's like taking off your wedding ring after the ceremony—freedom at last!

I managed to explain everything to him, even though he seemed to be more excited about my job than I was. It was almost like he had gotten a referral bonus for dragging me into this circus.

I told him, "I'm in an international process, American clients!" In my head, I was already picturing myself chatting away, helping Americans who had no clue what it took to get here—just to sit and type all day. But then it hit me: "Wait a minute, our IITians do the same thing, right? They fly across the globe, help Americans grow with their expertise, and everyone's like, 'Wow, look at them go!' So, if they can do it, why can't I?"

My friend burst into laughter, like I had just told him the funniest thing ever. "Yes, yes, you're right, man!" he said, laughing uncontrollably. And I couldn't help but join in.

"So, if they can do it, why can't I?" I said, grinning. "Besides, I'm about to help Americans grow... with my chat skills! Big proud moment!"

And the best part? The company would provide transportation. My friend could hardly contain his excitement. "Dude, you'll be sharing the cab with 3–4 others!" So much for independence, right?

I tilted my head slightly, putting on my best nerdy expression and said, "But hey, security is important." The company might have been giving me a ride, but at least they were making sure I wasn't roaming around like an unaccompanied adventurer.

My joining date was set for the 12th, and it felt like the universe was giving me a sign that maybe—just maybe—I could survive adulthood. Why? Because that meant I'd actually get paid this month.

Can you imagine? If the joining date had been after the 17th or 20th, they would have pulled the classic BPO move: "Congratulations! Your salary will arrive... next month!" My friend was practically doing a victory dance, as if he had just won the lottery. I couldn't help but wonder if he was secretly getting a bonus for mentoring me into this job.

The training shift was from 8 PM to 5 AM. Yes, nights. I almost laughed out loud thinking about how all my school teachers had said, "You're an owl!" and now, the office had confirmed it on paper. I was ready—nights were cool, right? Except, no one tells you that surviving the first few nights is like preparing for an endurance race. Coffee becomes your best friend, and the sun? Oh, the sun feels like your sworn enemy.

And here's where I clarify the most important thing about BPO life for anyone who might still be confused: Inbound vs. Outbound. Inbound is when the customers call you. It's a waiting game, and when they finally do, they're usually angry about something you had nothing to do with. Outbound is when you call customers and disturb their peace. You know those calls where you hang up the moment you hear, "Hi, I'm Puja from Domoshomo Insurance..." Yeah, that's outbound. Doesn't sound fun, does it?

Anyway, job? Done. Room? Rented—barely. Joining date? 12th. Now, I just had to survive my first night shift and officially enter the world of BPO life. And before you ask, yes, every month has a 12th, and in BPOs, there's always a fresh batch of dreamers who believe they're entering the golden age of job security. It's just how this whole insane system works.

TWO

Training Period – All Butter, No Bread

Waking up at 5 PM felt wrong, like I was living life backward. While others were wrapping up work and planning dinner, I was just starting my "morning" with a sleepy face and a confused brain. But hey, new job, new life, right? At least, that's what I kept telling myself.

Then came the real challenge—waiting for the cab. It was supposed to come at 6 PM, but by 7, I felt like I had been stood up. Was the driver coming from another country? Maybe he was lost in another dimension. Just as I started questioning my life choices, the cab finally arrived. The driver looked at me like I had kept him waiting. Amazing.

The cab itself was... an experience. Four people were already squeezed inside, looking like they had survived years of this night shift torture. I somehow fit myself in, folding my legs like a pretzel, and held onto my last bit of excitement. No one spoke. Just the sound of the engine and the deep silence of people who had made peace with their fate.

Driving through Gurgaon felt like I had stumbled into some alternate universe. No matter which route I took, I couldn't help but feel like I had to pass through CyberHub—like it was some sort of sacred pilgrimage. It was as if the city itself said, "You shall not enter without glimpsing this marvel of glass and steel!"

As I cruised past, the skyscrapers rose up like something straight out of a futuristic movie. And there it was, the building. From a distance, I could've sworn it was a copy of the Burj Khalifa. Wait—did I just say that? Oops, sorry! I meant to say, it almost looked like a very expensive, slightly shorter version of it. The city's beauty was blinding, with its never-ending lines of fancy cars, bustling streets, and people who looked way too important to be stuck in traffic, just like me.

But as I pulled up to the gate of my office, reality hit again. The excitement of driving through a "mini Dubai" quickly faded as I faced my next challenge: right at the gate—like life itself testing my patience. "ID card?" the guard asked, his expression as lifeless as my motivation to be awake at this hour.

I blinked. "Uh... first day," I said, attempting an awkward smile that I hoped screamed "trust me." The guard, clearly a veteran of fake excuses, raised an eyebrow so high it almost touched the security camera. "Entry register," he grunted, pointing at a book that looked like it had been passed down from the dinosaurs.

So, there I was, standing like a lost schoolboy, scribbling my name, phone number, and what felt like my entire autobiography in that oversized relic. The pen, of course, was as ancient as the book—barely working, threatening to give up on life at any moment. I shook it, tapped it, prayed to the gods of stationery, but nothing helped. Meanwhile, the guard watched me struggle like I was trying to crack a secret code instead of just writing my name.

After what felt like an eternity (or maybe just five minutes, who knows), I was finally allowed to pass. It felt less like entering my new workplace and more like crossing an international border—minus the luggage but with the same level of interrogation.

As I stepped inside, the office welcomed me with a blast of chilled air—ooo, the kind of air conditioning that made me want to throw my arms wide, like a Bollywood hero in slow motion, ready for my grand entrance. I could almost hear the dramatic music building in the background. But just as I was about to unleash my inner Shah Rukh Khan, the sound of a car horn snapped me back to reality. Honk, honk—right, I was at work, not in a movie. I quickly pulled myself out of my filmy illusion and tried to look like a professional.

And then, I saw it—the office.

It was lit up like a carnival, with so many lights it almost felt like I had walked into an over-ambitious wedding reception. Every inch of the place sparkled, as if the floors had been polished by some dedicated team of elves working overnight. The glass walls reflected the golden glow like I had stumbled into the headquarters of a multinational superhero league, and the floors were so shiny I could've sworn I saw the reflection of my slightly nervous self, and possibly my future career trajectory.

I glanced upwards, and through the glass windows, I saw people working—no, intensely working. They wore headphones that looked like they were plotting world domination, their eyes fixed on screens with an intensity I'd only seen in spy movies. I imagined they were decoding NASA-level equations or working on some corporate master plan to take over the world, but as I was about to learn, this was the dreaded "Voice Process." Yes, the BPO version of purgatory, where customers' problems scream louder than logic.

Thankfully, I'd been assigned to a chat process. No screaming customers, no headphones squeezing my brain out—just me, a keyboard, and text bubbles. It was as if someone had handed me a VIP pass to sanity. Life, for the moment, felt manageable.

But that peace didn't last long. I was wandering around like a lost tourist at a carnival, pretending I knew what I was doing, when my phone buzzed. "Hey, Madhav, where are you?" said an unfamiliar voice on the other end.

"Uh... who's this?" I asked, looking around like the caller might magically appear in front of me.

"It's Arjun. I'm your trainer!" he replied, sounding as enthusiastic as someone who had found their long-lost sibling.

At that moment, I felt an inexplicable connection, as though Arjun wasn't just a trainer, but my long-lost guardian angel. "I need you here ASAP," he added, giving me directions to the cafeteria.

I bolted up ten flights of stairs like I was auditioning for a fitness ad and finally reached the cafeteria, where I saw a girl sitting alone at a table. Her name, I soon learned, was Harshita. Arjun, who had somehow materialized out of nowhere, introduced us with a flourish, as if he were matchmaking rather than training.

"I need to check on the others. You two wait here," Arjun said, disappearing before I could process what was happening.

Left to our own devices, Harshita and I exchanged awkward smiles. It was the kind of smile you give when you're trying not to look like a complete fool. I'm pretty sure I could hear the awkwardness vibrating in the air. Harshita shifted in her seat, and I mimicked her, as if we were somehow in sync on this unspoken game of "Who Will Break the Silence First?" The answer: neither of us.

The tension hung in the air, thick enough to slice with a knife. Now, I've always believed in the golden rule of conversation: don't let the other person say 'ladies first'. If anyone dares to drop that line, a serious punishment is in order. Trust me, in this situation, 99% of the time, you're the one who has to start the conversation. Why 99%? Well, probably because once Supankha tried to go first... and ended up losing her nose in the process. Just kidding!!!!

And then, like clockwork, came the classic "So, where are you from?" and "How did you end up here?"—This keeps the flow natural and transitions smoothly!

She turned out to be a great listener—like, one of those people who nod at just the right moments to make you feel interesting. In ten minutes flat, we went from polite introductions to swapping numbers like seasoned friends. No, it wasn't some rom-com miracle—it was practical. After all, we were in the same training batch, and networking is key, right?

But as easy as it sounds, those ten minutes flew by like seconds. Two wannabe jokers sitting across from each other, cracking pointless jokes and grinning like kids who had just joined a circus. And perhaps, in a way, we had.

In the middle of our laughter and harmless banter, a new character entered the scene—a guy named Karan. And let me tell you, the moment he walked in, I could almost hear the opening theme of Mahabharat in my head. I mean, think about it: we already had Arjun and Madhav, and now here was Karan. The cosmic stage was clearly set for some epic drama.

Karan was... well, let's just say, a character straight out of a struggling actor's portfolio. Tall, lean, with hair that looked like John Abraham's early "wannabe rockstar" days. But it wasn't just his appearance—his entire vibe screamed, "I've been through the grind and survived to tell the tale."

As he spoke, his words carried the weight of someone who had seen it all—or at least wanted us to believe he had. "I've worked in this industry before," he announced, like he was some retired gladiator who had returned to the arena for one last fight.

To me, he seemed like the guy who had played this dangerous BPO game, lost a few battles, and yet decided to rejoin the chaos for the thrill of it. If I didn't know better, I'd have thought he was here to warn us about the perils ahead. But no, Karan wasn't a warning—he was the embodiment of the phrase, "Been there, done that, and still alive to joke about it."

I couldn't help but wonder if he was here for redemption or just another round of madness. Either way, I had a feeling this was just the beginning of the circus, and Karan was going to be one of its star performers.

As the clock ticked on, people began to trickle in, one by one, like contestants on a reality show nobody asked for. Remembering their names? Not a chance. Unless, of course, it was someone dramatic, like Karan, the BPO veteran who swaggered in as if he owned the place, or Harshita, the first familiar face who had already decided that being everyone's favorite was her life's mission. Everyone else?

For now, they were just "hey you" and "that person in the blue shirt," lost in the sea of new faces.

The team was... eclectic, to say the least. Harshita and Karan were graduates, wearing their degrees like badges of honor. Then there were the fresh-faced kids who had just finished their 12th grade and looked like they still needed their moms to help them cross the road.

And then, you had the overqualified folks—those who had clearly seen the inside of a classroom far too many times. With master's degrees hanging like a cloak of mild regret around their shoulders, they sat there with the expression of someone who had just walked into a life-altering mistake. "Why am I here?" they seemed to ask themselves. "Is this my rock bottom?"

The variety didn't stop there. Some people had the weathered faces of family men—probably already negotiating school fees in their heads. Others looked like they'd just walked out of a school assembly, still adjusting to the idea of working nights. It was a circus of strangers brought together by one thing: the promise of a paycheck.

Then there were the "veterans" of the BPO world. These were the ones who spoke like they'd fought wars on customer service calls. They knew all the tricks and weren't shy about telling everyone. And then, of course, there were the clueless ones—me included—wandering around with expressions that screamed, "What is happening?"

As I scanned the room, it hit me like a ton of bricks: this wasn't just a job orientation. No, this was a social experiment, one where the test subjects were stuck in a room together with nothing but awkward silences and half-hearted introductions. Everyone here had a story, and I was about to become the unwitting audience to each of them. It was only a matter of time before someone would regale me with their life's journey—from their childhood dog to their last college breakup.

But for now, I was just sitting there, trying to figure out if I was part of the cast or simply another confused soul in the audience, observing the chaos unfold. Was I in a reality show? Maybe. Was I a character? I had no idea. But either way, I was about to get a front-row seat to the madness.

Training period could easily be called a honeymoon period, and honestly, that wouldn't be wrong. Everything seemed perfect, everything was good. People from different states, who probably couldn't even manage a "Hi" from the girls in their class until yesterday, were now putting on their best "cool" act, like they'd been doing this for years. It was a bit of a transformation, really.

The girls, too, had undergone a total makeover. Those who used to get scolded by their mothers for the most trivial things were now strutting around with branded bags and accessories, flaunting them like they had just been crowned queen of the office.

As the training went on, we began remembering each other's names, probably because we were now all calling each other "friends." It was one of those moments where the word friend gets tossed around a little too casually, like it was some kind of corporate handshake. But let me warn you, the word "friend" in the BPO world can be more dangerous than a free lunch voucher—and trust me, you'll understand why as this story unfolds.

As time ticked on, we settled into the grind. Our rented rooms became our little sanctuaries – places where we could collapse after a long day and binge-watch whatever was trending, with zero worries of work (for those few hours anyway). The office, on the other hand, felt like a 5-star hotel with its AC-cool air that made you forget what real heat felt like. Saturdays and Sundays were our much-needed escape, and during the week, we were in product knowledge sessions, where we were spoon-fed everything about the client, the job, and the dream world they promised us after five years of hard work. Five years? The way they talked, I expected a chauffeur-driven car and a personal assistant named Gary to follow me around.

But here's where it got weird. No phones allowed. Yep, you heard that right. It was like stepping into a parallel universe where your phone wasn't just a tool—it was a liability. They weren't asking us to leave our phones at home. No, no. They wanted us to lock them away in a locker room like they were top-secret government files, sealed with a password only known to the higher-ups.

No outside food, no drinks, and absolutely no social media updates to remind you that you were missing out on your friend's exotic vacation while you sat there in fluorescent-lit captivity. Just... rules.

There was this story they told us, too, about why phones were banned in the first place. Apparently, some manager once made the "terrible mistake" of sharing floor data with someone outside the company. That's right—he thought it would be harmless. But no, that small slip-up ended with the client throwing a fit, and trust me, when a client's angry, the entire building can feel it. Since then, most BPOs have had a strict no-phone policy, fearing that customer data could be compromised. Even the trainers had to use their phones only under special, supervised conditions.

It felt like we were all secretly being trained to become spies on some covert mission, but instead of cool gadgets and high-tech espionage, our weapons were boredom and awkward small talk. The weirdest part? Every break felt like an intervention. Instead of checking our phones like normal human beings, we were stuck awkwardly chatting with colleagues we barely knew, pretending to care about their weekend plans or their dog's new obsession with chewing slippers. It was an uncomfortable social experiment—and we were the lab rats.

And then came the locker room. The place where your phone would go to "rest" for the day, crammed in a tiny locker as if it were some top-secret device that could never see the light of day. It was like we were playing a game of "Who Can Survive Without Their Phone the Longest?" Spoiler alert: it wasn't fun.

Still, we were all in the honeymoon phase.

As the days wore on and we spent more and more hours in this "no-phone" universe, we began to unravel the layers of each other's stories. And, if there was one thing that was universally shared among all of us, it was this: big, wild dreams. I'm talking about people practically carrying goalboards in their heads—visions of success that could put motivational speakers to shame. Some had stumbled into the BPO world just to kill time, others were here to escape the ghosts of a bad breakup (oh, you could spot those from a mile away—their eyes were always a little too distant, like they were still stuck somewhere in the past). Then, there were the ones who had been forced into this new chapter by the notorious "marriage ultimatum" from family. Get a job, or get married. Ah, the age-old parental love, wrapped in pressure and an uncomfortable deadline.

A handful had joined because they had been promised a salary hike—a shiny lure that worked every time. They had already spent years in the BPO grind, hopping from one to another, chasing the dream of just a little bit more.

But among them, there were one or two who were here for a different reason entirely. They were the ones who, in the absence of a father, had become the sole breadwinners for their families. The weight of responsibility pressed on their shoulders like an unspoken promise. It wasn't just a job to them—it was survival. And that? That kind of dedication? It melted anyone who heard their story.

And then there was me. I wasn't just dreaming small. No, my mind was on another level. I had grand plans to change the global economy— as I told you in the previous chapter, I even sat down with someone from the USA and discussed the gold-dollar issue over a cup of coffee. I had visions of world-changing discussions and deals that could reshape financial systems. But reality had a funny way of grounding me.

Everyone had their reasons, but we were all part of the same crazy journey now.

We were a team, a ragtag group of dreamers, some of us more polished than others, but all with that burning desire for something more. Slowly, we started becoming friends, even if some of us had to keep the "work-mode" on during lunch breaks. The best part? We were learning how to chat—and I'm not talking about casual texting. I mean the real art of work-related chatting. Apparently, if we managed to master the skill, we could boost sales and pocket some extra cash. That's when things really started to look interesting.

And then came the training. The kind where we were taught how to handle customers who, quite frankly, hated our client's product. Oh, the joy of speaking to someone who could barely hide their disdain. We had to act like we believed them—really believe them, or at least make it look like we did. We were basically trained to be convincing actors in a play where the script was always about "helping" people who just wanted to vent their frustration. So, yeah, while we might have been pretending to solve their problems, we were also pretending we cared. It was like walking the tightrope between customer satisfaction and staying polite enough to avoid getting yelled at. And trust me, in this world, acting like we were helping? It was an art form.

And then the real kicker came: overtime (OT) pay. Oh yeah. If we worked extra hours, we'd get paid even more. The idea of making more money by sitting in front of a computer and typing, it seemed like the ultimate hustle. My head started spinning, like, "Wait, what if I could actually make this work? What if I could really get rich doing this?"

And let's be honest—this wasn't just my greedy talking. This was the fuel that kept the entire BPO sector running. Scratch that—probably every sector. Nothing motivates a person quite like the sweet, intoxicating promise of extra income. Whether you were here to survive, thrive, or just avoid dealing with life outside work, OT had a way of making you stay.

I could already picture myself again in a fancy mansion, surrounded by gold and dollars, living the life of a billionaire. Of course, all I had to do was nail chat, sell, and somehow not get caught up in the chaos. Simple, right? Maybe I'd be the next big shot of the BPO world.

So there I was, lost in my dreams of billionaire life, thinking I had it all figured out. But life has a funny way of reminding you that things aren't as easy as they seem. Our primary classes had ended, and it was time to move on to the real stuff—getting a grip on our products. Simple, right? Well, not exactly.

In the middle of all this "learning," I got bitten by a mosquito. Yeah, a mosquito. And guess what? It wasn't just any mosquito. It gave me dengue. Dengue. Just like that. You know, like the universe was like, "Oh, you think you're going to be a millionaire? How about a little fever to remind you that you're still a mere mortal?"

Now, dengue doesn't just announce itself with a "Hello, I'm here!" It sneaks up on you, and it's got its own dramatic entrance. First, the room started getting cold. I mean, it wasn't the AC—it was like a random chill that took over my entire body. The yellowish lights in the training room dimmed slowly, like the universe was trying to set the mood for my misery. And then, I couldn't hear the trainer's voice properly. It was like the sound was fading, as if I was in one of those slow-motion movie scenes where everything's going wrong.

At that moment, I snapped and shouted, "Sir, I need water!" Now, Arjun, my trainer, was supposed to be the calm, composed guy, right? But in that instant, he looked at me like I just asked for the moon. I mean, it's the Kalyug, right? How can Arjun—our so-called 'super cool' trainer—deny me water? I'm practically melting here!

He looked at me with all the seriousness in the world, paused for a second, and said, "No, Madhav. You can't have water." And I was like, Wait, what?! Is this some new form of training? No water? Is this BPO boot camp or the Sahara Desert?

But it felt like time was moving in slow motion. I could barely focus on what was happening around me. I was just trying to stay conscious.

And then, as if the universe decided I'd had enough of my dream sequence, Karan appeared like some sort of hero. Background music intensifies: "Doo-doo-doo-doo, here comes the rescue!" Karan, looking like he was auditioning for an action movie, rushed over and said, "Madhav, bro, what happened? Let me walk you to the gate."

Meanwhile, the rest of the batch was looking at me like I was making it all up. You know, that classic reaction: "Is he really sick, or is he just pulling a prank?" Some people seemed like they thought

I was faking it, like I had suddenly discovered a new way to get attention.

But in the midst of all that confusion, Karan was there—taking me to the gate, making sure I wasn't just another victim of office drama. And that, in that moment, made me realize something important: "Does anyone here actually care? Or are we just playing this game of survival?"

It was a strange moment, one that made me think about the weird blend of caring and chaos that made up our BPO life.

So, here's the golden rule of BPO training—no breaks. Nope, not even if you're on your deathbed, not even if you have dengue, malaria, or the plague itself. You show up. Because apparently, they're not just training us for customer service; they're preparing us for some post-apocalyptic survival workforce where nothing—not even a zombie outbreak—should stop us from replying to customer queries.

But at this stage, you don't really feel the weight of it. You're still floating in the honeymoon phase of BPO life, where everything seems fun and new, and you haven't yet realized that "flexible work hours" actually means "your sleep cycle is about to be destroyed."

Meanwhile, I kept Arjun updated—not because he cared (he was a trainer, not a doctor), but because it was his sacred duty to pass information to the higher-ups, like some corporate messenger of the gods. Because in BPO, the process is simple: you get selected, you join, and then... you run for your life. That's the cycle. And trust me, it never breaks.

Now, here comes the fun part: After four days of battling dengue like a fallen warrior, I somehow managed to drag myself to the office. Was it my superhuman genes? My unbreakable spirit? Or just the fear of HR breathing down my neck? Who knows.

The moment I stepped in, Arjun's eyes widened like he'd just seen a ghost. "I didn't think you'd make it this far," he said, half-impressed, half-concerned. "You should've just rested. Production training has already started, and, well... you don't even know what we're doing yet."

But me, being the overconfident newbie, puffed up my chest and said with all the misplaced determination in the world: "No, sir, I'll cope up." Yep. Cope up. The legendary BPO phrase that defies grammar but defines survival.

Two days later, Arjun mysteriously vanished from the office. No warnings, no grand exit—just poof! Gone. Turns out, the mighty trainer who told me to 'just rest' had been taken down by typhoid. Now, I'm not saying it's funny, because obviously, being sick is not a joke, but honestly, part of me was like, "Well, well, well... look who's out of commission now. Talk about karma!"

I didn't exactly say it out loud because, you know, it's not nice to wish ill on people. But inside, I was kind of like, "Yeah, now you can update us on your situation instead of asking me all the time!" Funny how things turn around, right?

And then came the great trainer shuffle! After Arjun went down with typhoid, we got another trainer, whose name I don't even remember because, let's be honest, he didn't last long enough to make an impression. He came in, asked us our names, and then disappeared faster than a free pizza slice at a team lunch. It was like he was playing peek-a-boo with our training schedule.

Next up was Saloni. Now Saloni had this super enthusiastic vibe, like she was on a mission to change our lives—or at least make us believe she was. She started teaching us, and just when we thought we finally had someone consistent, poof! She vanished into thin air too. Maybe she found a better batch to train, or maybe the BPO training room just had a cursed door. Who knows? By this point, we'd started to treat every trainer like a guest appearance in our lives: "Enjoy it while it lasts; they're not here for long."

And then came Rohit. Ah, Rohit. The man. The myth. The nightmare. If Saloni was the sunshine of our brief training lives, Rohit was the thunderstorm that followed. This guy was something else. He wasn't a trainer; he was a drill sergeant reincarnated into the BPO world. He walked into the room with this look that said, "I'm not here to make friends." And boy, did he live up to that vibe.

Rohit was the kind of trainer who'd make you believe that training wasn't about learning—it was about surviving. The guy didn't just teach; he dictated. If we missed a single word or zoned out for even a second, his glare would make us question all our life choices. I swear, every time he walked into the room, it felt like we were being prepped for an army boot camp instead of handling chat processes. He was that one person who could suck the fun out of a Saturday off—without even being there.

The man had his own philosophy: "No pain, no gain." And by pain, I mean sitting through his intense sessions where he'd expect us to memorize product details like we were studying for the civil services exam. Need water? Too bad. Need to breathe? Ask permission first. It was like he was put on this earth to remind us that nothing in life comes easy—especially not in his class.

But, of course, Rohit had a soft spot... for himself. He seemed to have perfected the art of being a trainer without actually doing the hard work. While we were drowning in product manuals and mock chats, he'd casually scroll through his phone or sip on chai like a king savoring his empire. He was living proof that if there's a "malai" (cream) in the BPO training system, he had already scooped it all up.

Every now and then, we'd wonder: "Does he even know what he's training us for? Or is he just here to give us PTSD(Post-Traumatic Stress Disorder)?" But hey, the good part? His "army camp" vibes bonded us as a team. Nothing brings people together like shared trauma, and Rohit was the perfect catalyst for that.

And so, after countless nok-jhoks and sarcastic eye rolls, even Rohit—the mighty drill sergeant—came to realize that we weren't just a random collection of people from different backgrounds anymore. Nope. We were a team. A united force. A BPO Avengers squad, ready to take on whatever the corporate world threw at us (well, mostly). Our "united" status wasn't just a realization for us—it was a warning for him. It was like we collectively told him, "Rohit, go back to the ocean and bring us Saloni!"

And guess what? Miracles do happen. Saloni came back. Yes, our beloved ray of sunshine returned, and with her, so did some semblance of normalcy. Training resumed, and suddenly the air felt lighter—except for the fact that our training days were dragging on longer than a government project. The company, of course, didn't really care about us getting "fully trained." They just wanted us to hit the floor as soon as possible because, hey, clients don't pay for endless training—they pay for results. So, with just enough knowledge to be dangerous, we were being prepped to go live on the floor. "Fake it till you make it" was the unspoken motto at this point.

But before we step into the world of actual customers and real targets, let me take a moment to address something that became glaringly obvious during our training phase:

The culture of stress and its "solutions."

In the BPO world, what's alarming is how people deal with it. Here, drinking and smoking aren't just common—they're practically woven into the fabric of daily life. Need a break from the pressure? Light up a cigarette. Had a rough mock chat? Grab a drink after the session. These coping mechanisms became so normalized that they weren't just habits—they were part of the workplace culture.

I couldn't help but notice how many of my colleagues seemed to treat their bodies like disposable assets, sacrificing their health for a momentary escape from the grind. It was almost poetic in a twisted way—people killing their stress while slowly killing themselves. And what's worse? No one seemed to question it. This wasn't a problem; it was just how things were done.

What struck me the most was how casual it all felt. No one thought twice about showing up for training reeking of alcohol or stepping outside for a smoke every hour. It was the norm. A badge of honor, even. You weren't just learning how to handle customers—you were learning how to drown your anxiety in substances and call it "stress management."

But here's the thing: while everyone around me laughed it off, I couldn't shake the nagging thought in the back of my mind. How long could this go on? How long before these "solutions" stopped being temporary fixes and turned into permanent problems? It was like watching a slow-motion train wreck, and no one seemed to notice—or care.

And so, with these thoughts swirling in my head, our training came to an end. The company, of course, had no time to worry about such existential dilemmas. Their focus was clear: it was time for us to hit the floor. Ready or not, we were being launched into the real BPO world.

The training phase was over, and with it, our safety net vanished into thin air. Now, it was time to sink or swim—no more guided lessons, no more hand-holding. Just us, the screens, and the customers who probably had zero patience left.

I had heard whispers about the so-called Buddy-Up Session—a crucial 3-4 day period where fresh recruits would shadow experienced agents, watching them tackle customer queries like seasoned warriors. But thanks to our never-ending training delays (courtesy of trainer swaps that happened more often than weather changes), we had no time for that luxury. Instead, we were thrown straight into the battlefield with nothing but our scripts and sheer determination.

As I stepped out of the training room, a strange mix of relief and anticipation bubbled inside me. It felt like walking into a battlefield without armor—were we truly prepared for this, or were we just glorified crash-test dummies, waiting to see how hard the impact would be?

Little did I know, the real madness was only just beginning.

THREE

ON BOARD - "NESTING TIME"

The first look at the BPO floor felt like stepping into a whole new world. The sheer size of it was staggering—so big that for a fleeting moment, I thought to myself, You could probably play a game of football here. It was a hive of activity, buzzing with sounds of keyboards clicking, voices rising and falling, and the occasional burst of laughter. Yet, despite the energy, it felt overwhelming, almost like I'd been dropped into a world where everyone knew the rules except me.

Each corner seemed to have its own rhythm. One side was filled with people glued to their screens, their fingers flying across keyboards at lightning speed. They looked like they were in some sort of speed-typing competition, though their expressions showed anything but fun. I could already picture myself joining them soon, typing polite responses like, "Sure, I'll assist you with that!" while secretly rolling my eyes. Then there were the call agents—loud, animated, and deeply engrossed in their conversations. Watching them was like watching a live drama where every single one of them was the lead actor, delivering their lines with exaggerated enthusiasm or suppressed frustration.

As I took my first hesitate steps onto the floor, I could feel the eyes of the chat agents on me. It was as if they were silently saying,

"Run while you still can!" or maybe something like, "Oh great, another clueless rookie to join the chaos." Their expressions were a mix of amusement and pity, and honestly, it made me wonder if I had accidentally walked into a secret club where the entry fee was my sanity.

Some of them gave me quick glances and then went back to their screens, furiously typing away like they were in a battle with the keyboard. Others straight-up stared, probably thinking, "So, this is the new pigeon they've brought in to handle the madness? Good luck, buddy." The vibe was clear: I wasn't just entering a workspace; I was entering a battlefield where everyone was a seasoned warrior, and I was just the new recruit trying to figure out where to stand.

Our trainer announced, "Your nesting period begins here." And honestly, the whole "pigeon" thing started making way too much sense. She explained how we'd now handle live chats and use everything we'd been taught during training. Easier said than done.

The moment she finished, our entire team froze. We all just started looking at each other, like maybe someone else had a secret game plan. But nope, we were all equally clueless. Then, right on cue, the guy who had already handled chats before chimed in with a casual smirk, "Don't worry, it's super easy. I know how to do it."

Of course, he looked all confident, like he was about to save the day. Meanwhile, the rest of us were silently panicking, thinking, "Easy? Sure, maybe for you!" The atmosphere was a mix of fake courage and quiet dread, and I was just trying not to look as nervous as I felt.

Then our trainer introduced us to the support agents, who were called "PALs" for some reason. Honestly, I had no clue why they were called that. This was my first job, and half the terms they were throwing around made zero sense to me. All I knew was that I had somehow landed in this world of "BPO," which I'd always thought was just a fancy name for a call center.

To be honest, the BPO job didn't come with much of a reputation. I mean, who grows up saying, "When I grow up, I want to be an agent!" Right? Nobody. Even a tea seller these days becomes a startup icon, but if you're working in a BPO, people act like you took the easy way out. It was like the job came with this invisible label of "not good enough." Why that is or where this idea came from, I didn't know yet—but I could tell there was a story behind it, and I'd probably figure it out as I went along.

We grabbed our systems and, like nervous first-timers, decided to stick together for moral support. I parked myself next to Karan and Harshita, hoping the three of us could give each other some much-needed confidence. But, of course, the BPO gods had other plans. Karan's system refused to cooperate, and after some futile attempts at troubleshooting (mostly him just angrily hitting random keys), he gave up, muttered something under his breath, and moved to another corner of the floor. Slowly, the rest of the team also scattered like school kids trying to avoid the teacher's gaze, finding spots that felt less intimidating.

Then came the PALs—our official support agents. These were the people we were supposed to turn to if things went wrong during live chats. The twist? Both of them were named Ashish. Two Ashishes! It was like a sitcom setup waiting to happen. They introduced themselves, looking all serious and professional, but all I could think was, Great, now I have to figure out which Ashish to yell for when my system inevitably crashes.

With everything set, the "game" began. A few lucky souls logged in effortlessly, their screens flashing to life as they dived straight into their chats. The rhythmic clatter of keyboards and the low murmur of hushed conversations filled the air, a symphony of productivity. Others, like me, weren't so fortunate—our login IDs refused to cooperate.

At first, a tinge of disappointment crept in. Was this some kind of test? A glitch? Or just the universe's way of messing with me on my first day? But then, a realization struck: no login meant no work. No work meant an unexpected, unsupervised break. And suddenly, what should have been a problem turned into an opportunity.

Like any self-respecting newbie, I decided to make the most of it. Not by panicking or waiting helplessly at my desk—but by exploring. Purely for "educational" purposes, of course. With careful steps and a casual air, I wandered through the floor, absorbing the atmosphere, scanning the faces of my new colleagues, and trying to make sense of this world I had just stepped into.

As I wandered around, pretending to look busy, I stumbled upon an agent on a call. He had his customer on mute and was furiously cursing under his breath like a character straight out of a comedy sketch. Naturally, I couldn't resist asking, "What's up, man?"

He sighed dramatically, looked at me, and said, "This customer is frying my brain. I can't give him an earful on the call, so I do it on mute. Keeps me sane." He paused for effect and then added with a wicked grin, "Now I'm going to mess with him and ruin his night. He deserves it."

I stood there, both horrified and impressed. Wow, this is customer support at its finest. I'm learning so much already.

Just as I was trying to process this newfound "technique," I felt eyes burning into my back. It was my trainer, and she did not look happy. She motioned for me to come back, and as soon as I reached her, she gave me that look—the one that says, You're in trouble.

"What are you doing wandering around the floor?" she snapped.

"Just...observing," I replied, trying to sound innocent.

"Well, you can't," she shot back.

"Why not?" I asked, genuinely curious.

She sighed like she'd had this conversation a hundred times before. "Because someone here—their boss—doesn't like it when agents roam around."

And that's how I learned my first unspoken rule of the BPO floor: Even when you have nothing to do, you better look like you're doing something.

I don't know how, but by some miracle, my ID worked the very next day. No errors, no glitches—just a smooth login, as if yesterday's struggle had never happened. Finally, it was time to dive in, to get to work, to prove myself.

But as I settled in, something felt... off.

It didn't take long to notice the unspoken rule of the floor—our PALs were busy supporting the girls. And when I say "supporting," I mean attentively supporting, almost like personal assistants, anticipating their every need before they even had to ask. A quick answer here, a bit of troubleshooting there, an occasional reassuring nod—it was like they had been trained for this.

Meanwhile, the guys? Well, we were left to figure things out on our own. No extra help, no guiding hand, just a silent expectation to sink or swim.

Now, I wasn't about to overthink it or dive deep into any conspiracy theories, but it definitely caught my attention. I raised an eyebrow, feeling slightly out of place but shrugged it off. Still, I couldn't help but mutter, "Well, guess I'll just be here, doing my thing while everyone else gets VIP treatment..."

And yes, I said it loud enough for someone to overhear. Because why not? If I was going to be confused, at least I could share the confusion with the rest of the team.

So, there I was, sitting at my desk, feeling all confident, when—bam! My first chat popped up. My screen lit up like a Christmas tree, and suddenly, my hands were shaking like I had just downed three cups of coffee on an empty stomach.

Panic hit me like a ton of bricks. Oh no. Oh no. Oh no. My brain short-circuited. What do I do? What do I say? I had trained for this, right? Gone through the manuals, watched the demos, nodded along during orientation? And yet, in that moment, my mind was as empty as my savings account.

Instinct took over, and before I knew it, I had blurted out, "What do I do now?! Somebody, help!"—not in my head, not in a whisper, but loud enough for the entire floor to hear.

Heads turned. A few chuckled. One guy slow-clapped.

Meanwhile, my customer was still waiting. And in the cruelest twist of fate, they sent a message that read:

"Hello? Is anyone there?"

That's when it hit me—the irony of customer support needing support from the customer.

Then, the answer came from the heavens in the simplest form: "Just reply, simple." Oh, right, replying! How could I forget? I felt like I had just cracked the Da Vinci code. But then, I turned around to double-check if anyone had heard me losing my mind, and that's when I saw her. And oh my god... She looked like the missing piece of my heart, the kind of girl that BPO myths are written about.

The kind of girl HR warnings are issued for. An angel, but like, the call-center edition. She had the corporate ID card, and the expression of someone who had already dealt with at least three idiots before . I was about to become the fourth. I was so stunned, I forgot what I was supposed to do.

Instead of asking for help, like any sane person would do, my mouth decided to take over. I opened it and blurted out, "Hello! How are you? I'm Madhav, the new join."

She blinked at me, I blinked back,
The lights flickered, the air turned slack.
The AC sighed in a tired old tone,
Yet in that moment, we stood alone.

She shot back, snapping me out of the daydream I was happily lost in—"Reply as early as possible, duffer!"

Before I could even react, she pulled up a chair next to me, settled in like she owned the place, and started typing away. My chat? Hijacked. My role? Reduced to watching in stunned silence.

She handled everything like an absolute pro—quick, efficient, and completely unfazed, while I sat there wondering how she made it look so effortless.

And that's when it hit me.

This. This is why PALs are always so eager to help with girls' chats. It's not about strategy or teamwork. It's pure survival.

But hey—just kidding! I mean, we men are totally happy with a little helping gesture too, you know. We appreciate the backup. It's just that sometimes... we might accidentally need it more than we admit.

So, there she was, typing away like she was born for this, talking to the customer with complete confidence, while I was just sitting there like a deer caught in headlights. Every tap of her keyboard was like the sound of a drumbeat, and in my mind, it was a full-on soundtrack playing in the background. The music? Oh, it was dramatic. Think slow-motion "Mission Impossible" with a hint of romance—because why not add some intensity to the mix?

As she expertly navigated the chat, I was stuck in a trance, staring at her like I had just witnessed the first human capable of multitasking. She was calm, composed, and effortlessly professional. Meanwhile, I was there sweating like I'd just run a marathon and had no idea what to do next. My brain was screaming, "This is your first chat! Say something!" But my mouth had clearly decided to take a vacation.

And there she was, typing faster than I could process the information, all while maintaining perfect eye contact with the screen—like she was a superhero in the world of customer support. Meanwhile, I was trying to figure out what planet I was on, getting lost in the rhythm of her keystrokes, occasionally snapping out of it to realize, "Oh right, I'm supposed to be doing something too."

Every time she pressed "send" and moved on to the next customer, I swear I heard the sound of a gong in the background, like a reminder that I was still here, doing absolutely nothing.

So, there I was, lost in my own little world, staring at her like I had just discovered a new species, when she suddenly looked up from her screen and hit me with the most casual yet deadly line: "Could you please look at the screen instead of checking me out?"

I swear I nearly jumped out of my chair. My face went bright red. I fumbled out, "Uh, my trainer is Saloni... but I think it should be you, honestly." She raised an eyebrow, probably thinking I was insane, and casually replied, "Why not?"

Then, she casually hit me with another question, "And who's your PAL?"

"Uh, Ashish," I stammered, feeling like I was slowly digging myself into a hole. She nodded as if she was taking mental notes, chatting away with the customer and answering my endless stream of questions like it was nothing. Honestly, it was like watching a pro magician pull off trick after trick, and I was just standing there, wondering if I could ever be that smooth.

And then it hit me—I just wanted to talk to her all day. I mean, how could I not? Her voice was so soothing, it could probably put an entire army of babies to sleep. Her face? Glowing like she had a secret glow-up serum. I was this close to asking for skincare tips.

But just as I was about to say something (probably something totally stupid, knowing me), she stood up and started walking away. It was like the music in the background turned into slow motion, and I could feel the dramatic "Noooo!" building up in my head. Without thinking, I blurted out, "What's your name?"

She turned, flashed a smile so powerful it could have ended wars, healed heartbreaks, and maybe even convinced my landlord to lower the rent. And then, with the kind of mysterious charm you only see in movies, she said—"You'll find out."

Oh, come on! I swear on my ex—crush, I mean—this actually happened.

And just like that, she walked away, leaving me standing there like a total mess of a human being, wishing I could go back in time and at least have a decent conversation with her. Instead, I was left with nothing but a heart full of "what ifs" and an overwhelming urge to never leave my desk again.

Do you remember that school love feeling? When your brain was overloaded with things to say—grand speeches, perfectly crafted one-liners, maybe even a whole love letter—only for you to end up saying... "Hi."

Yeah, that.

But no, idiot! That's not what this is. Why am I going so deep? This isn't some dramatic love story with background music playing. It's just a normal conversation... right? Right?!

And yet, here I am, stuck in analysis mode, as if decoding the meaning of "You'll find out" is more important than finding the Wi-Fi password.

Saloni, my trainer, walked over with that look—the one that instantly told you, "You're in trouble." If looks could be report cards, mine would have had a big, fat red FAIL stamped across it.

She pointed straight at me and said, “Stop staring at the girls and focus on your chat. You know you need to make at least one sale during nesting to pass, right?”

I blinked. Stared at her like she had just asked me to recite Shakespeare backwards. "You must be kidding! I’m here to do chats, not sell stuff!"

Saloni didn’t even flinch. “Nope. One sale. At least. And you’re going to do it.”

This had to be a joke. "But that’s not what I was hired for!" I protested. "You hired me for chats, not sales!"

Saloni, clearly immune to my panic, just shrugged. “Doesn’t matter. One sale. It’s part of the deal.”

And that’s when I knew—I had no way out. The rule was simple yet cruel: Make a sale, or fail. Oh, and just to add an extra layer of suffering, customers also had to rate us at least 4 or 5 stars at the end. Anything less? Basically career suicide.

Now, I had zero idea how to sell anything. But at this point, I had no choice. I took a deep breath, cracked my knuckles, and entered that chat with the same nervous determination as someone trying to talk their way out of a speeding ticket.

And you know what?

Somehow, miraculously, at the end of the chat—I got a 5-star rating.

FIVE. STARS.

I nearly jumped out of my chair in celebration. My first-ever successful chat, and it was perfect! In my head, I was already mentally thanking the girl who had taken over my chat earlier, thinking,

"You just made my day... and possibly my career."

I looked around to make sure nobody saw me trying to hold back a ridiculous grin. “Thanks, universe,” I whispered, feeling like I had just won the BPO lottery.

(Customers don’t even realize it, but their one little rating can literally make or break someone’s career. Like, before dropping a

0-star rating for fun, just take a moment to imagine the poor soul sitting in a chaotic, stress-filled environment, running on caffeine and hope, trying to survive.

That one rating? It's not just a number. It's the difference between "Congrats, you passed!" and "Pack your bags, buddy."

So, dear customers, before hitting that unnecessary low rating, just remember—on the other side of that screen, someone's career is on the line.)

The 7-day nesting period was supposed to be our training ground—our chance to prove ourselves by getting good ratings and, most importantly, making at least one sale.

Sounds simple, right?

Yeah, that's what I thought too. Until I realized this wasn't some easy onboarding session with free coffee and motivational speeches. Nope. This was BPO boot camp. Except, instead of push-ups and obstacle courses, you had to master the art of selling things you didn't believe in and convincing customers who didn't want to be convinced.

It was survival of the fittest.

If you didn't get a sale, you were basically on thin ice. If you didn't get good ratings, you were practically falling through that ice. And if you messed up on both? Well... let's just say your career was one bad chat away from vanishing into thin air.

This wasn't just about learning the ropes. It was about proving we could handle real customers, real pressure, and real rejection—all while pretending we were totally fine and not on the verge of a meltdown.

Oh, and the company? They weren't just watching—they were waiting. Because in this world, you weren't just hired; you had to prove you deserved to stay.

But here's the kicker—the sale just wasn't happening for me. My ratings? Decent. My enthusiasm? Hanging by a thread. But no matter how hard I tried, closing a deal felt like trying to convince a cat to take a bath. Even my PAL, Ashish, was putting in the effort, throwing out sales pitches like a street vendor trying to sell sunglasses during a thunderstorm, but customers just nodded (virtually) and disappeared into the abyss.

And then, right in the middle of my sales misery, I saw her again—the girl who had taken over my first-ever chat. Without thinking (because thinking clearly wasn't my strength at that moment), I sprang up from my chair like someone who had just sat on a thumbtack, wildly waving my hands like a fisherman exaggerating his latest catch.

"Oye, oye! Come here!" I called out, as if I had just discovered a life-altering secret.

She turned, looked straight at me... and then strolled away like I was a "Lose Weight Fast" ad she couldn't close fast enough.

I stood there, hands still in midair, frozen in pure betrayal. Wait... did she just pretend she didn't know me?

I felt my ego take a massive hit, and I slumped back down in my seat, thinking, Seriously? This is how it's gonna go? But then, just as I was about to wallow in my own embarrassment, she walked over to me, and I could tell she was trying not to laugh.

She stood next to me, looked me up and down, and asked, "What's up? Why are you shouting like a madman? This isn't a circus, you know."

I was totally caught off guard. But, before I could apologize, I just blurted out, "I can't make a sale. I have no idea how to do it!" I probably sounded like a lost puppy at that point.

She chuckled and then said, "No worries. Just give me a second. I'll talk to my TL, and I'll come back to help you. Wait here, alright?"

And just like that, she left, leaving me with a mix of relief and confusion. Was I getting help? Or was this just another "you'll figure it out" moment? Either way, I felt like I had just been saved by a BPO angel—one that wasn't afraid to call me out but also didn't leave me hanging.

She came back after getting the go-ahead from her TL, and like a BPO wizard, she helped me make that sale. And let me tell you, when that sale finally went through, I was practically doing cartwheels in my head. "Thank you, thank you so much!" I couldn't stop thanking her. It felt like I had just won the BPO lottery. That was the moment I knew I had officially crossed the nesting hurdle and had made it into the world of customer support.

I rushed to Saloni and told her, "I did it! I finally made the sale!" She was genuinely happy for me, but of course, the real question was, what was her name? And where did she go?

I asked Saloni if I could take a break and go outside to clear my head. She, being the kind trainer she was, gave me the green light. And like a man on a mission, I set off looking for my BPO savior. And there she was—sitting, minding her own business, looking like an angel who had just saved my job. I walked up to her, gave her a big smile, and said, "Thank you again for helping me out!"

And then, without missing a beat, I added, "Hey, how about a cup of coffee sometime?"

Because let's be real, after pulling off a legendary ignore-and-smirk combo, she at least owed me a coffee—or at the very least, a sympathy biscuit for my bruised ego.

She smiled with her friend sitting next to her and, in a teasing tone, said, "Oh, coffee with you? Why, by the way?"

I was totally caught off guard, and with a mix of nervousness and gratitude, I stammered, "Well, because you helped me... this won't go unappreciated!" I was still trying to play it cool, but inside, I was probably screaming, Please say yes!

But, of course, fate had other plans. Just as I was about to look for my chance to continue the conversation, her TL walked over and, with a slightly stern look, said, "Why are you standing here? Go to your system!"

I didn't even know she was her TL! Man, in the BPO world, age really is just a number. I was expecting the TL to be some older, serious-looking person with a permanent frown and a coffee addiction, but nope—here was this young girl, casually being the boss. It completely threw me off.

But hey, why not? When people start working at 18, climbing the ladder fast is bound to happen. One day you're struggling to spell "escalation," and the next, you're the one handling them.

And on top of that, I had to think about my own PALs. They had looked like the kind of guys who'd be managers based on their experience, but nope, I was in for a surprise! Seems like BPOs don't follow the usual script—anything can happen!

As I started walking away, feeling a little defeated and honestly embarrassed, she suddenly called out, "Wait! Give me 5 minutes; I'll join you after taking a break."

For a moment, I stopped in my tracks, unsure if I'd heard her right. Did she just say she'd come along? My inner monologue went something like: Wait, what? Is this real? Do people actually get breaks in this place? Or is this just my lucky day?

I turned back, nodded quickly (probably too quickly), and tried my best to look cool, but let's be real—inside, I was grinning like a kid who just got extra candy. Five minutes. Just five minutes, Madhav. Play it cool. Don't mess this up.

And then, finally, she came out. With a slight adjustment in her tone, she said, "So, coffee? Let's go."

I swear, in that moment, I felt like I'd just won an award. My inner voice was screaming, Oh my god, maybe my recent haircut actually worked this time! Trying to keep my excitement in check, I casually nodded and walked beside her, though my brain was running laps in celebration.

Meanwhile, back at the floor, my teammates were buried in chats, typing away like their lives depended on it. And there I was, sipping coffee with her, feeling like I'd cracked the ultimate BPO jackpot. I mean, how often do you get a chance like this?

While we were talking, I finally worked up the courage and asked, "So... now that we're having coffee, will you tell me your name?"

She smiled, took a sip of her coffee, and casually said, Kavya.

It was such a simple name, yet it felt like it carried a certain charm, especially when she said it. For the next few seconds, I couldn't even focus on the coffee—I was just repeating her name in my head like a secret mantra.

After returning from coffee in a surprisingly good mood, I couldn't help but notice something odd about the BPO floor. It was as if stress was written into everyone's job description. People were running around, typing like their keyboards owed them money, or talking into headsets with voices that screamed frustration. I mean, does anyone here even know how to smile?

Before I could dwell on it too much, my trainer Saloni appeared, her sharp eyes locking onto me like a hawk. "Madhav! Where were you? You can't keep disappearing like this. Don't make it a habit, okay?" she scolded, but her tone carried more irritation than actual anger. "Go to the meeting room. I'll join you in a bit."

With a sheepish nod, I walked toward the meeting room, where a mix of agents—some relieved, others visibly stressed—were waiting. Nesting wasn't over for everyone, and the tension in the room was thick. But honestly? It didn't bother me. My nesting was cleared, and more importantly, I had found my reason to stay in this chaotic world.

A few minutes later, Saloni entered the room with her usual authoritative stride, the kind that could make even the most confident agent sit up straight. "Alright, listen up!" she announced, clapping her hands together like a coach about to give a halftime speech. "For those of you who have cleared nesting—congratulations! You'll now be assigned to your respective teams. And yes, your Team Leads (TLs) will guide you from here."

The room reacted in the usual BPO fashion—a mix of half-hearted clapping, nervous glances, and that one guy who looked like he had just lost a bet. Some were celebrating their newfound freedom, while others sat there staring at the floor, mentally calculating their remaining days of job security.

Saloni started reading out the team assignments, and then it happened. "Madhav, your TL will be Mohak."

Mohak. The name struck a chord in my brain, and suddenly, Kavya's words from our coffee break came rushing back.

"Mohak sir? Oh, he's the best TL on the floor. The others? Useless or always angry. You're lucky if you get Mohak."

Hearing that, I had laughed at the time. "Oh, why not? I mean, do you really think this would make me happier than drinking coffee with you?" I had said, throwing in my best attempt at a flirt.

Kavya had just rolled her eyes and scoffed, "Oh, please. Flirting doesn't suit you, Mr."

And now, sitting in that meeting room, I couldn't help but grin. Jackpot.

While some agents groaned at their TL assignments, I sat there, looking smug like a guy who had just won a free upgrade on a flight. By pure luck—or maybe divine intervention—I had landed with the most coveted TL in the BPO.

As I scanned the room, I noticed two more selected faces—Karan and Harshita—also waiting for their names to be called. Karan looked mildly amused, like he already knew the corporate circus we were stepping into, while Harshita sat upright, looking ready to conquer the world—or at least her chat queue.

This was it. The real deal. No more mock chats, no more training modules where we pretended to understand company policies. This was where it truly began.

For the first time, I thought, Maybe... just maybe... I might actually survive this.

At that moment, I also knew the reason why everyone here was so on edge, constantly irritated, and borderline dramatic wasn't just the job pressure—it was the money.

If our batch didn't pass—or at least if more than 80% didn't make the cut—our trainer wouldn't get their incentive. No extra money, no celebration, just another failed batch on their record.

So yeah, money was the reason behind all the chaos, the panic, the sudden mood swings of our trainer. Not some noble mission of shaping us into perfect employees. Nope. It was all about that extra paycheck.

And the work itself? Oh, they had already cracked the code. They knew exactly how to convince customers, how to spin stories, how to make a refund sound like a favor instead of a right.

Basically, the real training wasn't just about handling chats—it was about learning how to fool both the customers and the clients.

Now, all we were curious about was Mohak and his team.

Was he really the legendary TL everyone hyped up? Would his team be a dream squad or a chaotic mess? More importantly—would we actually get some breathing room, or was this just the beginning of another horror story?

FOUR

MOHAK AND HIS TEAM

The day began like most in the BPO—chaotic, caffeinated, and buzzing with barely-contained mayhem. Before the actual work started, there was the mandatory team meeting, a daily ritual every agent on the floor knew all too well. It was that sacred moment where the day's strategies were laid out with great enthusiasm, targets were declared with forced optimism, and everyone engaged in the grand performance of pretending they had their lives together. Meanwhile, I sat there thinking, "Dude, we just have to solve customer queries. Why the drama? Such a waste of time."

(Now, I get it—we need meetings, strategies, and all that serious business talk. But come on, I was new there! My biggest strategy was figuring out where the coffee machine was. So stop judging my thoughts.)

I walked into the meeting room with Karan, my training partner-turned-colleague-turned-survivor-in-arms. We had endured the nerve-wracking training period together, battling cryptic scripts, robotic roleplays, and an instructor who seemed to derive joy from our confusion. And now, by some stroke of luck—or perhaps a cruel joke by the HR gods—we had landed on the same team. Mohak's team.

Mohak's name carried weight on the floor, spoken about like he was some kind of legend among exhausted agents. People made him sound like a customer service genius, someone who could calm even the angriest caller with just a sigh. I expected a big personality—maybe a sharp suit, a powerful presence, or a speech about how to crush our targets.

Instead, I saw Mohak. A bearded guy in a plain t-shirt and jeans, standing there like he had seen every problem in the world and couldn't be bothered by any of them. No grand gestures, no loud speeches. Just a look that said, "Let's finish our work and leave on time."

Next to him stood Diljit, our SME (Subject Matter Expert). No, no, not that famous Diljit Dosanjh, but somehow a 3-4 copy of him. If Mohak was the calm leader steering the ship, Diljit was the mischief-maker with a map—one that was probably upside down—throwing sarcastic directions at everyone like a stand-up comedian lost at sea. Diljit was the kind of guy who could roast you so smoothly that you'd walk away feeling flattered, only to realize five minutes later that you had just been thoroughly insulted.

"Ah, new faces," Diljit said, smirking as Karan and I sat down. "Now, before you believe anything I say, let me remind you—whenever an SME or a TL tells you that their team is the best, take it with the same confidence as a political party claiming victory before election results. We're all the best, apparently. It's just something we've learned to say." "Welcome to the team. You're lucky, you know. Mohak's team is the best on the floor. No pressure, though. If you mess up, we'll just blame each other. Team spirit, right?"

Karan shot me a look, his eyes screaming, "What have we walked into?" I barely suppressed a laugh. This was going to be interesting.

Mohak, leaning casually against the table like a wise sage who had seen it all, let Diljit bask in his self-appointed spotlight before finally deciding it was time to restore order. "Alright, team. Let's focus. Today, we're aiming for high promoter scores and solid sales. Basically, let's convince customers they need things they never thought about until they met us. Customers come first—always. Then, it's every agent for themselves. Treat every chat like it's the only one that matters. Keep it professional, keep it simple ,which I assume means typing with proper punctuation while hiding my existential crisis.

His voice wasn't loud, but it carried weight. Even the agents who were usually restless sat up straighter. Mohak had this way of commanding attention without even trying.

Diljit, never one to miss a chance to add his brand of wisdom, jumped in with his usual flair. "And don't forget, folks—upselling isn't just a skill, it's an art. Slide in that product or service suggestion like it's a casual conversation. You know, like, 'Oh, by the way, have you considered spending more money?'"

The room erupted in chuckles, partly because it was funny, but mostly because we all knew it was painfully true. Diljit had a way of keeping things light, even when the targets felt daunting.

As the meeting continued, I realized why this team was so highly regarded. There was a rhythm to it—a balance between Mohak's quiet authority and Diljit's witty energy. It wasn't just about numbers or targets; it was about creating an environment where everyone felt motivated to do their best—or, let's be real, greedy to get more money.

Toward the end of the meeting, Mohak turned his attention to me and Karan. "Welcome to the team," he said, giving us a small smile—that rabbit smile I would never forget. "You'll find that we're more than just coworkers here. We work hard, but we've got each other's backs. If you need help, don't hesitate to ask."

"And if you don't need help," Diljit added, "still ask. I need the entertainment."

The meeting wrapped up, but I already knew—I had landed in the most unpredictable, ridiculous, and oddly perfect team on the floor.

As the hours passed, I started to see what made this team so special. There was a sense of camaraderie, of shared responsibility. Everyone knew their role, but no one hesitated to step in when someone needed support.

At the end of the shift, we gathered again for the debrief. Mohak stood in the same spot, his hands tucked into his pockets, listening intently as team members shared their experiences. Wins were celebrated, struggles were acknowledged, and even the funniest customer interactions were shared. Yes, there were plenty of hilarious moments—like how the problems customers faced often became our inside jokes, how we unintentionally ruined someone's night by giving half-baked assistance, or the art of strategically disconnecting chats just in time to avoid a negative rating. It was all part of the game, and somehow, it made the madness of the shift worth it.

It was in that moment I realized how lucky Karan and I were. This wasn't just a team; it was a family. Mohak wasn't just a leader—he was someone who inspired respect through his actions, not just his words. And Diljit, with all his sarcasm, was the glue that kept things lighthearted, even on the toughest days.

As we left the room, Karan nudged me. "We really lucked out, didn't we?"

"Yeah," I said, smiling. "This is going to be something else."

The first few days in Mohak's team as newcomers were... well, let's just call it an advanced course in social awkwardness. The existing team didn't exactly roll out the red carpet or shower us with a grand welcome. As a team, they were the best—no doubt about that. But as welcoming hosts? Let's just say, if they ever threw a party, even they wouldn't want to attend. It wasn't personal, probably. Maybe they weren't the "new-people-enthusiastic" type. Maybe they had trust issues. Or maybe, deep down, they just knew that welcoming new employees meant more people to share the coffee machine with.

But hey, isn't that how all great relationships start? With a little tension, a few awkward stares, and an unspoken battle over who gets to use the best desk?

Honestly, the team was less of a professional workforce and more of a daily soap opera—complete with drama, plot twists, and characters who deserved their own theme music. If I started naming every single person here, this chapter would probably become more boring than it already is. So, let's just pick two. Maybe they'll even pay me for featuring them. Just kidding. (Or am I?)

Now, before you start thinking these are real people, let me assure you—these names are purely fictional. Or at least, that's what I'm going to say to keep your attention.

So, the two lucky winners today are Anshuman, the guy who could sell ice to an Eskimo, and Sahil, the guy who could single-handedly tank the team's score with the efficiency of a malfunctioning chatbot.

If Anshuman was the team's rocket ship, blazing through targets and making impossible sales look easy, Sahil was the gravity ensuring we never got too carried away with success. Just like in every BPO, in every team, there are always those agents, one who is absolute legend at sales and customer support—charming, confident, and capable of convincing a customer to buy things they didn't even know existed. And then.... The ones who either look perpetually confused or are so mentally checked out that you can almost hear their soul whisper, "Bro, just log me out permanently."

Probably, they've figured out a deep, hidden truth—more sales mean more sins. Oops.

Their partnership was a cosmic joke—one breaking records, the other breaking spirits. Some said they existed solely to maintain balance in the universe. Others believed HR just kept Sahil around to keep Anshuman humble. Either way, watching them work was like watching a magician and his accidental saboteur.

Of course, I wasn't particularly concerned about them at the start. Why would I be? I had Diljit, the resident sarcasm expert, to roast me every other minute, and Mohak, the ever-calm team leader, to save me when things got too intense. So, my social circle felt pretty complete at that point.

But as time passed, things started to shift. Slowly but surely, we began cracking inside jokes, sharing memes like they were classified intel, and bonding over the absolute absurdity of customers asking the kind of questions that made you question humanity itself. Turns out, it's not that hard to become part of a team if you're willing to do three things—drop the ego, fake a few laughs at bad jokes, and most importantly, share your snacks during breaks. Because let's be real, nothing builds trust faster than a packet of chips in a BPO.

I remember one such moment of frustration vividly. I was juggling multiple chats, each customer seemingly more eager than the last to verbally assassinate me. Just when I was about to lose my sanity, I looked up and saw a girl with fiery red hair. And trust me, she looked so effortlessly cool that for a second, I considered signing up as an organ donor just to offer my eyes to science for witnessing such perfection. As fate would have it, she was the girlfriend of one of our team members but somehow the best friend of nearly everyone else. Typical.

That was just the kind of environment our team had—nobody cared whether your "person" was around or not. Your partner wasn't just your business; they were the team's unofficial hot topic of discussion. One minute, you're peacefully taking chats, and the next, your significant other is the subject of an intense roundtable analysis featuring experts in gossip, sarcasm, and unsolicited opinions.

My seniors, especially the ever-wise Mohak, started teaching me the ropes of the job. "Customer support isn't easy," he said. "But if you think of the customer as just another human being—one as flawed and frustrated as you—it gets manageable." Of course, there were some... unfiltered gems of wisdom too.

"Indian customers?" Sahil mused one day, reclining in his chair like some kind of overworked philosopher. "Chaotic. Absolute rollercoaster. American customers? Slightly better. At least they say thank you before ruining your day."

Mind you, this was coming from the same guy whose sales numbers were so low, even the system probably felt bad and stopped counting. But hey, even broken clocks are right twice a day.

And honestly, his words got me thinking—this isn't just BPO wisdom, this is life advice. If you're out there looking for a partner, make sure they know how to talk. Because when fights happen (and they will happen), good communication is the only thing keeping your relationship from turning into a cold war. Choose wisely, my friends.

In the midst of all this, I realized that Mohak's team wasn't just about the work. It was about the people. Sure, the characters I met could fill an entire sitcom, but over time, they became my sitcom. And though the journey was just beginning, I knew it was going to be one heck of a show.

But for now, let's start with Anshuman and Sahil—the chaos crew that made life in the team anything but boring.

Sahil was the oldest resident of Mohak's team—both in tenure and, quite possibly, in spirit. I don't know how, but every single person in that team swore he had been around since the dawn of time. Some joked that Sahil had been part of the team even before Mohak had become the team leader. Others insisted he belonged to the Stone Age, conveniently skipping through evolution straight to the BPO. If you asked him how long he had been here, he'd just smirk and say, "Long enough to know all your mistakes before you even make them." Honestly, at one point, I half-expected HR to find his fossilized remains buried under the office desks.

At first, I thought they were just exaggerating. You know how teams like to mess around and build these legendary backstories for people who've been around too long. But, well, time has a funny way of proving people right. It wasn't until I started sitting next to Sahil during chats that I realized he might actually be an ancient relic. The man had a way of saying things that didn't just sound old-school—they sounded downright alien.

For example, once, while I was struggling with a particularly stubborn customer who refused to understand even the most basic instructions, Sahil leaned over and muttered, "Patience, young one. Customers are like coconuts—tough on the outside but filled with the same predictable nonsense inside." I blinked at him, unsure whether he was giving me advice or just hungry. Another time, when I was losing my mind over back-to-back escalations, he simply sighed and said, "In my time, we didn't fear escalations; escalations feared us."

I wasn't sure if he was trying to motivate me or if I had just accidentally joined a cult.

The more I worked with Sahil, the more I realized he existed in some strange, paradoxical space—he never hit his targets, never took things too seriously, but somehow, he always had just enough wisdom to sound like he knew what he was talking about. He was like one of those characters in an ancient scroll, who sat in a corner watching the world burn, sipping tea, and occasionally dropping life lessons that didn't make sense until three weeks later.

And, of course, this was the guy handing out life advice like free samples at a supermarket. One day, out of nowhere, he looked at me and said, "Listen, if you ever get into a relationship, make sure your partner knows how to argue properly. Not just shout—really argue. Because trust me, when things go bad, the only thing keeping your relationship alive will be your ability to fight smart."

I stared at him, confused. "Uh... what?"

Sahil just shrugged. "Think about it. If both of you know how to argue well, at least your fights will be productive. If not, you'll end up arguing about arguing. That's the real nightmare."

And just like that, he leaned back in his chair, as if he had just solved world hunger.

I wasn't sure what disturbed me more—the fact that he was making sense or the fact that I was actually considering taking relationship advice from a guy whose longest commitment was probably his yearly subscription to a food delivery app.

When I first left home to join this job, I had grand dreams—big ones. The kind where you picture yourself in a high-rise corner office, making billion-dollar deals while sipping on overpriced coffee. I thought I was setting out on a journey to conquer the corporate world, to climb that fabled ladder straight to the top.

And then, I met Sahil.

Sitting next to him made me question whether anyone else in this place was even thinking that far ahead. Because Sahil? He didn't want to climb the ladder. He wanted to set it on fire and walk away. His grand plan wasn't to rise through the ranks of the BPO—no, his dream was to escape it entirely.

"I'm gonna start my own business one day," he'd declare confidently between handling chats, as if the universe had already taken notes. The irony? He never had the time to actually plan how to start that business because he was too busy handling back-to-back customers at the BPO.

And that wasn't just Sahil's story—it was the story of countless others here. People who never planned to be in a call center but found themselves stuck, just waiting for that 'one day' when they could leave. The problem? Life didn't come with a pause button. There was always another shift, another paycheck to chase, another month that blurred into the next.

But despite all his flaws—and trust me, Sahil had plenty—there was one thing no one could deny: the man knew how to handle customers. He might have been hopeless at hitting his sales targets, but when it came to dealing with the trickiest, most unreasonable customers, Sahil was nothing short of a legend.

It was mesmerizing, really. His calmness, his sharp wit, and the effortless way he turned even the angriest customer into a cooperative human again—it was impressive. There were times when I would pause my own chat just to watch him work his magic. If a customer came in breathing fire, Sahil would smirk, throw in a well-placed joke, and somehow, by the end of the conversation, the same customer would be apologizing for being rude.

And that's why, no matter how much we teased him, the team respected him.

In an industry where burnout was more common than lunch breaks, where employees came and went like the changing seasons, Sahil had stayed. Not because he loved the job, but because he knew how to survive it. And that, in itself, made him irreplaceable.

Looking at him, I couldn't help but wonder—was this what the BPO did to people? Kept them tied down in a cycle of "one more month" until years slipped by unnoticed? And yet, even as I had these deep, existential thoughts, Sahil would crack a joke or tell some absurd story that had the whole team laughing.

He might not have been the hero we deserved, but he was definitely the one we needed to keep things interesting.

And then, there was Anshuman.

If Sahil was the team's ancient relic, Anshuman was the shiny new toy everyone envied. He was younger than me, hadn't even graduated yet, and somehow had the best sales numbers on the floor. The guy made closing deals look as easy as breathing. It was almost infuriating.

According to Sahil, Anshuman had grown his beard in this BPO itself. The moment Sahil realized this, it became his life's mission to troll him endlessly.

"You see, kids," Sahil would say, wrapping an arm around Anshuman like some old sage, "this boy walked in here fresh-faced and innocent. But the BPO changes you. Now, he's got stress lines, a five o'clock shadow, and an existential crisis brewing inside him."

Anshuman would just roll his eyes, but I could see the smile tugging at the corners of his lips.

The team was full of personalities like this—people who had stumbled into this world by accident, each with their own dreams, their own struggles, and their own way of making this chaotic job just a little more bearable.

And somehow, despite the frustration, the targets, and the endless stream of customers asking the dumbest questions known to mankind, I was starting to feel like I belonged.

Despite being the youngest, Anshuman carried himself like the most seasoned agent. He was annoyingly friendly, greeting everyone with a big smile and a polite tone that made you wonder if he was secretly running for president. But don't be fooled—his kindness didn't stop him from sarcastically reminding you that he was better.

"Sales is an art," he told me once, grinning after I struggled through a chat. "You're just in your abstract phase right now." I couldn't even argue because, well, he wasn't wrong.

Sahil loved teasing Anshuman about everything, from his sales skills to his beard, but even he had to admit that the kid was a natural. "He'll sell water to a fish," Sahil once muttered, half-annoyed and half-impressed. Anshuman just grinned and said, "And make them ask for a subscription plan."

If Sahil brought the chaos, Anshuman balanced it with charm—and a healthy dose of sarcasm. Together, they were the two extremes of the team, and honestly, it was entertaining just watching them.

As the days passed, Karan and my friendship grew naturally, like an inside joke that kept getting funnier. At first, Karan was just another colleague—someone I exchanged quick nods with while logging in for the shift. But before I knew it, he had become my go-to person for everything, from handling cranky customers to figuring out which cafeteria snack wouldn't betray my stomach.

Karan had been in this BPO environment longer than most, and it showed. He had a way of maneuvering through the system like he had cheat codes for the job. If there was a shortcut to make life easier, Karan had already discovered it, tested it, and probably improved it. While I struggled to keep my cool with irate customers, he had a signature move—smoothly escalating the chat so professionally that even the team leader wouldn't blink twice. It was like watching a magician at work.

Sales? That was my battlefield. Problem-solving? That was Karan's kingdom. I could convince a customer to buy something they didn't even know they wanted, but Karan could take the most complicated issue and break it down so simply that even the customer felt like a genius by the end of the chat. Between the two of us, we had an unspoken partnership—I made the sale, he made sure they didn't ask for a refund.

We became so inseparable that just starting our shifts on time wasn't enough—we'd come in 30 to 40 minutes early just to talk. And it wasn't about work; our conversations were so fun and engaging that we'd forget we even had a shift to do.

When it came to breaks, we didn't exactly follow the rules. Instead of the usual short ones, we'd take our own—sometimes stretching them to two, even two and a half hours. In a nine-hour shift, that was a lot of time spent just laughing, joking, and goofing off. But honestly, that's the only way to survive in a BPO. The irony is, you can't make it in this job unless you have someone just as inseparable from the madness as you are.

Technically, BPOs only allow one hour of break time, but we operated on a whole different level. We'd stretch the limits, pushing the clock and sometimes logging out late, because honestly, what was the point of rushing when you were having fun? The other team leaders started noticing, and let's just say, the complaints about our "extensive breaks" began to pile up.

But then, something unexpected happened. Mohak, our team leader, who was never exactly closed off but also not the kind to casually joke around with us, slowly started easing into our vibe. He wasn't the type to join in on pointless chatter or waste time on anything that wasn't strictly work-related. At first, he kept his distance—watching, listening, maybe even trying to figure out how Karan and I managed to spend an entire shift laughing while still getting our tasks done. He wasn't unfriendly, just... reserved. Professional. The kind of guy who'd acknowledge you with a nod but wouldn't stick around for small talk.

But something shifted. It started small—an amused smirk here, a half-suppressed chuckle there. Then, one day, it happened. We were mid-laugh over something completely ridiculous when Mohak, instead of shutting us down, just shook his head, exhaled sharply, and said, "I got your complaint." We froze for a second, thinking, Oh, great. Who snitched? But then he continued, his expression unreadable. "I don't care," he said, pausing just long enough for us to exchange confused glances. "Until and unless you do your work properly."

And that was it. That was the moment we realized we had won him over. It wasn't an open invitation to slack off—he was still our team leader, after all—but it was as close to a green light as we were ever going to get. The message was clear: Do your job, and I'll look the other way on the rest.

From that point on, "Mohak Sir" became "Mohak Bhai." The change was subtle but undeniable. He no longer just tolerated our antics—he became part of them. He didn't always jump in, but he never stopped us either. It was like we had unlocked a hidden level of trust, an understanding that as long as we got the work done, we were free to make the job our own.

And it wasn't just about fun. Just like how Netaji's backing could make the goons fight over territory, Karan and I quickly realized that having Mohak on our side gave us something invaluable: breathing room. The pressure of the job didn't suffocate us anymore. The rules, once rigid, now had a little more flexibility. The late nights felt less like a burden and more like a shared experience.

With Mohak in our corner, we weren't just surviving the BPO life—we were thriving in it. Not by being the best employees, but by making the job something we could actually enjoy. And in a place where burnout was just part of the package, that was a win in itself.

Just as we had Mohak on our side, Mohak had his own secret weapon—Manish, the manager. And let me tell you, when you've got both the team leader and the manager in your corner, life in the BPO becomes a lot more flexible. There were no more complaints or reprimands. We could pretty much do whatever we wanted with our shifts, as long as we didn't completely slack off.

It was, without a doubt, the most glorious misuse of someone's name in the history of BPOs. But what can I say? When you've got the right people backing you up, you take full advantage of it. Our shifts turned into a game of "How late can we log out without getting caught?" and "How long can we extend our breaks while looking busy?"

And honestly, as much as it meant bending the rules, it never really felt wrong. After all, with Mohak's support and Manish's approval, we were basically living the dream. What can I say? When you're in the right place with the right people, sometimes the rules are just... suggestions.

And it wasn't just Mohak, our TL, or even Manish, our manager, who had loosened up around us. Even Anil, our floor coordinator—the guy whose job was to keep an eagle eye on agents' logins, ensuring no one was slacking—was with us too. Normally, the FC is the person you avoid when you're trying to sneak in a few extra minutes off the phone, the one who makes sure every second of your shift is accounted for. But in our case? Let's just say he wasn't exactly keeping tabs on us the way he probably should have.

Now, in most BPOs, playing with a stress ball, tossing it around, or even keeping one at your desk is a big no-no. It's seen as unprofessional, a distraction—something that takes away from the all-important metrics. But here? Here, things were different. Not officially, of course. No one came out and said, "Sure, go ahead and turn the floor into a playground." But when your FC, TL, and even your manager aren't stopping you, it kind of becomes an unspoken rule that some rules just don't apply.

And maybe it was because of the absurdity of our shifts. We worked with American customers, which meant our schedules were never fixed. One month, we were adjusting to nights, surviving on caffeine and the hum of computers. The next, we were suddenly on day shifts, pretending like our bodies weren't completely out of sync. That's the thing about BPOs—24/7, always ready to assist, no matter what. Which, when you really think about it, leads to some ridiculous contradictions.

Like, imagine feeling suicidal and finally finding the courage to call a helpline, only to hear that it's available Monday to Saturday, 10 AM to 8 PM. Oh, you need help outside those hours? Sorry, buddy, try again tomorrow. Meanwhile, a BPO? We're open all the time. Whatever the crisis, whatever the time—someone, somewhere, is awake and working.

Oops. Where was I going with this? Right, back to the point.

So yes, our FC was with us. Our manager wasn't even around for this shift. And our TL? Well, he wasn't just allowing it—he was right there with us, playing along. It wasn't just a team anymore. It was something else entirely—a perfectly balanced mix of rule-bending, survival, and finding a way to actually enjoy the madness of it all.

In our team, there was one person whose name I learned not to mention lightly—Puja. Now, Puja wasn't just another BPO agent blending into the crowd. No, she had built a reputation so legendary that even the new hires were warned about her within their first week. She was the kind of person who could charm you into a conversation so effortlessly that before you knew it, you'd be nodding along, completely at ease. And then, just when you thought she was simply being friendly, she'd casually slip in the real reason she had approached you.

"Hey, yaar, can you lend me some money? Just a little—I'll return it as soon as I get my salary."

It always sounded harmless, innocent even. But there was a catch—once the money left your hands, it might as well have disappeared into a black hole. Puja wasn't borrowing money. She was collecting it. And getting it back? Well, let's just say, unless you had a direct line to the afterlife or a fully functional time machine, your chances were slim.

I still remember the first time she tried it with me. I was new, fresh-faced, and still naive enough to believe that colleagues helping each other out was just part of the job. My wallet was halfway out of my pocket when, out of nowhere, Diljit—the SME who had an uncanny ability to appear exactly when needed—swooped in like a seasoned detective stopping a rookie from making a fatal mistake.

"Don't give her anything," he said firmly, grabbing my hand before I could hand over the cash.

I blinked at him, confused. "Why?"

He sighed, shaking his head like a teacher disappointed in a student's lack of street smarts. "Because, my friend, you won't get it back. Ever. Not unless you've got a time machine lying around somewhere."

I must have still looked lost because he leaned in, lowering his voice as if he was revealing one of the great untold secrets of BPO life.

"In this place, people will do anything for a day off and for borrowing money," he explained. "Some will tell you their grandma's in the hospital. Others will swear their pet dog is on life support. But let me tell you something—if you ever hear about a so-called dying relative, just nod and smile. It's all part of the game."

He paused for effect, then added, "And Puja? She's the grandmaster."

I looked over at Puja, who had already moved on to another unsuspecting agent, flashing her signature 'trust me' smile. And that's when I realized—this wasn't just a one-time thing. It was an art form.

And the thing is, Puja wasn't alone. The office was full of Pujas—agents who could spin the most heart-wrenching stories at the drop of a hat just to convince you to part with your hard-earned cash. There was always someone whose father was in the hospital, someone whose mother needed emergency surgery, or someone whose phone screen had tragically cracked, and they just needed a little money until salary day. The stories varied, but the end result was always the same—you'd never see your money again.

It was one of those unwritten lessons you had to learn fast in the BPO world. Because while handling customers was the official job, handling people? That was the real challenge.

After that day, I made a silent promise to myself—I wouldn't fall for it again. No matter how tragic the story, no matter how convincing the performance, I would nod, smile, and keep my wallet firmly in my pocket.

And with that, another chapter of my BPO life came to a close—richer in wisdom, if not in cash.

FIVE

LOVE : A BLUETOOTH CONNECTION

Love in a BPO is like a Bluetooth device—quick to pair when in range but just as swift to disconnect the moment distance creeps in. It thrives in proximity, feeding off shared breaks, stolen glances across dimly lit workstations, and the quiet understanding that only those who endure the same grueling shifts can truly share. It's an ecosystem where bonds are formed in the glow of computer screens, under the hum of fluorescent lights, amidst the symphony of ringing phones and hurried keystrokes.

Here, romance operates on borrowed time, slipping in between calls and team huddles, flourishing in the stolen minutes of a chai break at 3 a.m. or whispered conversations in stairwells where the cameras don't reach. It's a delicate dance between transient joys and unspoken realities, a connection built not on grand gestures but on the simple comfort of having someone who understands the exhaustion in your voice without you having to say a word.

Promises are made—some earnest, others uttered in the heat of a moment, both vulnerable and aware of their fragility. They often crumble under the weight of shifting schedules, mounting targets, and the relentless churn of an industry designed for impermanence. Love here isn't about forever; it's about surviving the moment. It's about clinging to warmth in a cold, impersonal environment, about finding solace in someone who knows exactly how it feels to be trapped in an endless cycle of log-ins and log-outs, KPIs and escalations.

And yet, for all its fleeting nature, love in a BPO is intense. It exists in a paradox of connection and detachment, where emotions run high but are often left unspoken, buried beneath professionalism and the constant ticking of the clock. It's a microcosm of the BPO itself—fast-paced, temporary, and transactional, yet laced with a bittersweet nostalgia when the shift ends, the floor empties, and the glow of the screens fades into darkness.

Because when morning breaks and the outside world beckons, those midnight confessions, stolen kisses in break rooms, and whispered "take care" messages dissolve like mist—leaving behind nothing but memories and the soft echo of a love that was, for a moment, just enough.

Kavya and I had settled into an unspoken routine, one that neither of us had ever put into words but followed religiously nonetheless. Every day, without fail, we'd step out together for our breaks, weaving through the maze of cubicles and glowing computer screens as if drawn by an invisible thread. Saying hello with just a glance had become second nature—no need for words when a flicker of the eyes across the floor spoke volumes. It was a silent language of familiarity, a small but comforting certainty in a job that offered little else.

Sometimes, I'd hand her a chocolate, and on other days, she'd slip a toffee into my palm—little tokens of affection, chosen not for grandeur but for practicality, because budgets in a BPO life were as tight as the shift schedules. A chocolate or a toffee wasn't just candy; it was a gesture, a reminder that amidst the monotony of endless chats and performance metrics, someone was thinking about you. And yet, even this small act of warmth came with its own set of hurdles.

Why is this important, you ask? Because in that BPO, outside food wasn't allowed. As ridiculous as it sounded, the rule stood firm—no matter how long your shift was, no matter how exhausted you felt, the company had its own way of controlling even the smallest aspects of your life. It was just one of those things, one of the many policies that made you question the system. I mean, someone should really tell them that this BPO work is soon going to be taken over by robots and chatbots. The industry was changing, automation was creeping in, and one day, the very people enforcing these petty rules might find themselves replaced by algorithms with no need for tea breaks or meal restrictions.

But until that day came, shouldn't they at least respect the people who kept the wheels turning? The ones who sat through grueling shifts, handling multiple chats at once, managing frustrated customers through text, hitting unrealistic targets, and pretending they weren't exhausted? It wasn't much to ask for—a little dignity, a little humanity. But maybe that was the real irony of working in a place like this. You spent your days typing out solutions for strangers, resolving their issues through chat windows, yet no one really listened to you.

And so, in defiance of the rules, we kept up our little exchange—Kavya's toffees, my chocolates—because sometimes, even the smallest acts of rebellion felt like victories.

Outside of the office, we were nothing. There were no late-night calls, no long messages, no promises of meeting outside. What we had existed only within those walls, under the glow of computer screens and the hum of air conditioning. And after some time, our timings changed too, slowly widening the gap between us. We still talked whenever we got the chance—sometimes during overlapping breaks, sometimes through a quick message before logging out.

But soon, I started realizing that this wasn't unique. This was something everyone did there. I mean, it was normal. People connected, shared jokes, and found comfort in fleeting conversations, knowing well that most of these bonds wouldn't last beyond the shift. It was just part of the BPO rhythm—temporary, convenient, and easily replaceable, much like everything else in that world.

I remember the story of Akshay, a guy who had a girlfriend outside the office, yet somehow, that never stopped him from trying to impress Komal. He'd take over her chats whenever she looked exhausted, flashing a casual smile as if he were doing something heroic. "Go take some rest, my queen," he'd joke, and she would laugh, knowing exactly what was happening but never calling it out. It was a game, one they both played without ever acknowledging the rules.

Akshay was an SME, someone people relied on for guidance, but in this little bubble of office life, he was just another guy looking for something to hold onto during long shifts. Komal, on the other hand, had a boyfriend outside of work, but that didn't matter in the world they had created for themselves. Inside the office, they were different people—people who weren't bound by relationships that existed beyond these walls. They pretended to be a couple, calling themselves a "cheers" couple, as if their bond was just a casual toast, a fleeting celebration of shared moments that wouldn't last past their log-out time.

This was something Kavya had once told me about, and at that moment, it all started to make sense. Relationships in the BPO weren't always about love or commitment; sometimes, they were just about survival. About finding someone to laugh with, to share the monotony, to make the never-ending shifts feel a little less suffocating.

The BPO world had this odd sense of duality, where relationships were often built on proximity and convenience, rather than real emotions. The line between what's genuine and what's temporary blurred, and sometimes, you just had to go along with the flow to survive.

Sometimes, it feels to me like the concept of love these days doesn't really exist anymore. It's as if people don't even bother to invest emotions into anything real. Instead, they just make do with whatever time they have, forming connections in whatever fleeting moments they can find. The idea of commitment or deep affection seems lost, replaced by temporary distractions that fit into the chaos of their busy lives.

Maybe it's the environment—like in a BPO, where everything is fast, transactional, and constantly changing—that makes it feel like love is just another part of the job, something that fades as quickly as it appears. You can't help but wonder: is this all we have now? Quick connections that don't last beyond the shift? It's hard to tell if this is what people actually want or if they've just accepted it as the norm.

Kavya, with that ever-mischievous grin of hers, turned to me and said, "Madhav, listen, love doesn't exist here, so you better be careful." Her voice carried a mix of amusement and warning, as if she had seen too many people fall for the illusion, only to crash and burn.

For a split second, I felt like thanking my lucky stars. I mean, honestly, this was exactly what I was planning to say! It was almost like she had read my mind, but in the most... 'nasty' way possible. She said it with such confidence, as if it were a universal truth, something she had accepted long ago. And here I was, thinking the same thing all along.

I couldn't help but chuckle to myself. "Well, looks like I'm not the only one who figured that out," I thought. Love in the BPO world? Ha! It was like looking for Wi-Fi in the middle of nowhere—sometimes you'd get a signal, but it was weak and unreliable, and you knew it was going to disconnect any second. People here didn't fall in love; they fell into patterns, into temporary companionships that lasted only as long as the shifts did.

I just smiled to myself and thought, "This... this is going to be fun."

Turning to her, I nodded and said, "Yeah, sure. I don't believe in love either. This whole culture is a mess, and I know I'll find my love when the time is right." My words came out casually, but deep down, I wondered if I really meant them. Maybe I did. Maybe I had already seen enough to know that emotions here were like coffee—strong, addictive, but eventually, they turned cold.

Kavya threw her head back and laughed, the kind of laugh that made you feel like she knew something you didn't. "Of course," she said, "you're a dashing man and talkative too! You don't need to please anyone; the right one will come." She paused, giving me a knowing look, then smirked. "And that's what happens when your heart's been broken—you start spouting philosophy."

I raised an eyebrow and let out a small laugh. Was she right? Maybe. Or maybe we were all just pretending not to care, shielding ourselves behind cynicism because that was the easiest way to survive here.

I couldn't help but laugh at that. It was true—when you've been through enough, you start to sound like a life coach, whether you mean to or not. Experience has a funny way of making you philosophical, especially in a place like this, where emotions were often reduced to fleeting moments between chats and breaks.

But just as I was enjoying our lighthearted banter, Kavya suddenly dropped a bombshell, completely shifting the tone of our conversation. She was resigning. Her last working day was approaching.

For a moment, I just stared at her, trying to process what she had just said. "Wait, what? You're leaving? Why resign?" I asked, still struggling to wrap my head around it.

She let out a sigh, the kind that carried both relief and uncertainty. "Because I want to pursue an MBA."

Ah, there it was. The classic exit plan in the BPO world. It made sense. Most people here didn't intend to stay forever. They either climbed the corporate ladder or used the experience as a stepping stone to something bigger—an MBA, a government job, or simply a way out of the monotonous cycle.

I shrugged, nodding slowly. "Ohhh... I didn't know that."

But despite my casual response, I felt a strange sense of unease. It wasn't like I hadn't seen people come and go before—this place was a revolving door. You'd build connections, share laughter, have inside jokes, and then, one day, they'd be gone. That's just how it worked. Still, this time felt different.

Over time, Kavya and I had built something—a bond that didn't need labels, just an unspoken understanding. And now, the thought of her leaving made me realize how accustomed I had grown to her presence. I wasn't devastated or heartbroken, but there was this lingering feeling of... something. A mild sting, maybe.

And, to be honest, I knew why. Unlike many others in this chaotic ecosystem, Kavya was different. She wasn't like Puja, who had casually asked me for money as if it were just another workplace favor. Kavya never played those games, never used people, never indulged in the typical office manipulations. Maybe that's why her leaving hit me a bit harder than I had expected.

Maybe—just maybe—it was the respect she carried. Or the fact that, in a world where everything felt temporary, she remained true to herself. Even in the madness of it all, she never lost her essence. And that? That was rare.

Mohak and Karan had reached that level of friendship where they probably knew me better than I knew myself. It's funny how that happens. You spend more than half your day with the same people, sharing meals, complaints, inside jokes, and before you know it, they've somehow cracked the code to your personality—even the parts you haven't fully figured out yet.

So, naturally, when I told them the whole Kavya story, their reaction was instant and explosive. They didn't just laugh—they howled. The kind of laughter that rings in your ears before it even happens, the kind that makes you want to take your words back the second they leave your mouth.

Mohak, ever the troublemaker, leaned forward with a mischievous smirk and raised an eyebrow, like a detective who had just solved the biggest case of his career. "Are you in love?" he teased, dragging out the words as if he was savoring every bit of my misery.

I rolled my eyes, scoffing at the very idea. "No, not at all."

But the moment the words left my mouth, a tiny, annoying part of my brain whispered, Are you sure?

I mean, I had Kavya's number. What more could I possibly want? We texted sometimes. We shared a few good conversations. But that was it. That was the decency level of mine, right?

Before I could finish my internal debate, Karan, with his oversized ego and an equally oversized sense of humor, decided to throw in his two cents. And, of course, he had to do it in the most theatrical way possible.

"Oh, you're definitely in love with Kavya."

He said it with such absurd confidence that for a second, I almost believed him.

That rascal. That absolute menace of a friend had this weird superpower—he could plant thoughts in your head, and once they were there, they just stuck. Like an annoying song you didn't even like, but suddenly you're humming it all day. That's what his words felt like.

I let out an exasperated sigh. "Seriously?" I asked, now thoroughly flustered. "I'm not in love. Stop messing with me."l

But, of course, Karan wasn't done. He could smell my discomfort, and that only fueled his enthusiasm. He grinned like a man who had just won a bet.

"Madhav, you're a walking rom-com waiting to happen."

I groaned, running a hand down my face. At this point, I was genuinely considering changing my number, moving to another country, and possibly faking my own death—anything to escape Karan's relentless "love guru" routine.

Because the worst part?

Now that he had said it, I couldn't stop thinking about it.

As Kavya's last day at the office crept closer, something inside me shifted. It wasn't sadness, not exactly, but an unsettling feeling that sat heavy in my chest. A sort of emptiness, like a balance being disrupted in ways I couldn't quite explain. We weren't even on the same shift most of the time, and our conversations—though frequent—had never ventured into anything deeply personal. Yet, somehow, the idea of her absence felt like something I wasn't ready for.

The weirdest part? I had her number. I could text her whenever I wanted. Call her, even. Technically, nothing was really ending. If I missed her, all it took was a simple message. And yet, that knowledge didn't comfort me. If anything, it made things worse. There was something different about seeing her every day—the unspoken familiarity of a shared space, the casual interactions that never needed an invitation. The way her presence colored the monotony of workdays, making them feel a little less dull.

I kept telling myself, It's fine. People leave jobs all the time. And yet, I couldn't shake this feeling of loss. Like something significant was slipping away, even though I had no real claim over it. Over her.

Maybe it was the predictability of our routine, the way she'd tease me about my coffee addiction or the way she'd roll her eyes at terrible office jokes before breaking into that half-smile. Maybe it was knowing that after tomorrow, those small moments wouldn't happen anymore.

I wasn't sure what I felt, only that it lingered long after I told myself it shouldn't.

Maybe that's just how the BPO world works. Everything is temporary—shifts, coworkers, friendships, and even the so-called relationships. People bond over shared struggles, late-night chai breaks, and inside jokes born from exhaustion. But the moment someone walks out of those office doors for good, it's like none of it ever really existed.

It's funny how affection in a place like this only seems to exist within the building—within the walls of that claustrophobic office, surrounded by the constant hum of machines and the never-ending pings of chats. Outside, everything evaporates.

One day, you're laughing over silly conversations and stolen breaks. The next, you're just left with a bunch of "Goodbye" messages on Slack—messages that feel so impersonal, so disconnected, it's almost as if the bond never happened at all.

And maybe that's what bothered me the most.

Not that Kavya was leaving, but that this is how things always end here.

And yet, as the day neared, I felt like I was losing a piece of that chaos, that rhythm of conversations during breaks, that occasional exchange of chocolates or toffees... that weird BPO connection that never really had a name but was somehow always there.

I guess it was just the office drama playing its part—just a phase, right? But for a split second, I actually felt like there might be something more than just a passing chat or shared coffee breaks. Maybe that's what makes BPO relationships so confusing: You're never really sure if it's something real or if it's just the chaos of the job. Either way, at least it kept things interesting.

And so, the end was here. Our friendship, built on stolen moments during breaks and countless chats, was about to become another fleeting memory in the BPO world. As much as I tried to act indifferent, there was a weight in my chest that I couldn't shake off. Kavya was leaving, and with her, she was taking a part of the rhythm that had kept me going in this chaotic, robotic environment.

She wasn't just a colleague or a friend; she was the girl who helped me with my first sale when I was struggling to even get a proper sentence out during a chat. She was the one who stayed patient when I panicked and made sure I didn't mess things up. Kavya wasn't just a coworker—she was someone who made this place, this job, feel a little less mechanical and a little more human.

On her last day, as the hours passed, I felt an odd sense of dread. The kind that comes when you know you're about to lose something you took for granted. When the time finally came to say goodbye, I stood there, trying to find the right words, but everything felt too small, too ordinary for the moment.

I wanted to thank her for everything—for the help, the laughter, and the moments that made this place bearable. I wanted to tell her how much I appreciated her for being a part of my journey, for the chocolate exchanges, the honest advice, and the quiet camaraderie we shared. But words felt inadequate.

So, instead of fumbling for the right words—words that would never quite capture the weight of this moment—I stepped forward and wrapped my arms around her in a tight hug. It was instinctive, unplanned, but it felt right. My way of saying everything I couldn't put into words.

She tensed for the briefest second, as if caught off guard, but then she melted into the embrace, holding onto me just as tightly. There was no hesitation, no awkwardness—only warmth, only understanding.

"Thank you," I whispered, my voice almost cracking. It was such a simple thing to say, yet it carried so much more. Thank you for the laughter. Thank you for the late-night conversations that made long shifts bearable. Thank you for the small moments, the unspoken support, the way you made this place feel a little less like just another job.

She pulled back slightly, just enough to look at me, and smiled—a bittersweet smile that said she understood. That she felt it too. Then, without a word, she hugged me even tighter, as if trying to pour all the unspoken emotions into that one moment.

And just like that, I let her go.

Some bonds aren't meant to last forever, but that doesn't make them any less real. They leave a mark—a quiet, invisible imprint on your heart. A reminder of the people who walked into your life, changed it in ways you never expected, and made it better, even if only for a little while.

As I walked back to my seat, my mind still lingering on the warmth of that hug, I blinked rapidly, trying to push back the sting in my eyes. But it was too late—one rogue tear had already escaped, trailing down my cheek before I could wipe it away.

That was when Mohak, my ever-reliable team leader, caught sight of me. His timing, as always, was impeccable.

He let out a loud, amused laugh, the kind that could be heard across the floor. "Are you crazy? This stuff keeps happening here," he said, grinning like someone who had seen it all in the chaotic world of BPOs. "People come, people go. It's just how it is."

I rolled my eyes, trying to act like his words didn't affect me, but I knew he wasn't wrong. The nature of this place was transient—colleagues leaving, new ones replacing them, conversations fading, memories getting buried under fresh deadlines and new faces.

And yet... this felt different.

I let out a small chuckle, shaking my head. "Yeah, yeah, I know," I muttered, sinking into my chair. But even as I said it, I couldn't shake the feeling that this time, it wasn't just about someone leaving a job.

This time, it felt like something a little more personal.

Mohak wasn't just a TL; he was more like a big brother to me. He was the kind of leader who didn't just give orders but stood by you through everything—offering advice, cracking jokes, and making sure you never felt lost. Whether it was a tricky escalation or just dealing with the randomness of office life, he was my backup, my guide, and honestly, the reason I didn't lose my sanity here.

Seeing my glum face, he decided to pull me out of it in his classic style. "You know what? Karan got rejected by another girl," he said with a sly smirk.

That was it—I couldn't stop laughing. Poor Karan! His love life was like a stand-up comedy routine, full of endless rejections, and every new episode was somehow funnier than the last.

And just like that, our trio was back in action—me, Mohak, and Karan, laughing like idiots and letting go of the stress of the day. Mohak had this knack for turning even the worst situations into something bearable.

Just as we were laughing at Karan's never-ending rejection stories, a girl walked up to us, looking a little impatient.

"Hey, can you check my chat? My shift is over, and I have an exam to catch," she said, tapping her watch like we were on borrowed time.

Now, of course, she had a valid excuse—education is important and all. But where's the fun in just saying yes?

I grinned. "Sure, but first, what's your name? You know, just in case I need to write 'helped a pretty girl today' in my daily report."

She rolled her eyes but smirked. "Prisha."

I chuckled and turned back to Prisha. "Well, Prisha, consider your chat checked. But fair warning—you now owe me a coffee. It's the official BPO rule, I don't make them."

She laughed, shaking her head. "Nice try, but I think I'll just say thanks instead."

"Ah, rejection," I sighed, looking at Karan. "Now I know how you feel, buddy."

And just as she walked away, the system popped up—"New device connected."

A new chat for her, another story for us, and another day in the chaos of BPO life.

SIX

DARK CHRONICLES

Working night shifts in a BPO is like stepping into an alternate reality, a world that runs on a schedule completely opposite to the rest of society. While your friends and family wake up to start their day, you are just getting into bed, hoping for a few hours of uninterrupted sleep before the cycle repeats. The natural rhythms of life—daylight, social interactions, regular meal times—begin to slip away, leaving you feeling disconnected from the world outside.

One of the biggest struggles of working the night shift is missing out on important moments. Birthdays, weekend plans, and family gatherings slowly become rare luxuries rather than regular experiences. Your schedule is so out of sync with everyone else's that even the simplest of conversations become difficult to maintain. You wake up in the late afternoon only to find a flood of missed calls and messages from people who were active during the day. By the time you get a chance to respond, they are either too busy or already asleep. It is an isolating experience, one that social media only amplifies. Scrolling through your feed, you see your friends enjoying brunch, attending parties, or relaxing on vacations while you sit under the artificial glare of office lights, trying to sound cheerful to an irate customer complaining about a delayed package. There is a deep sense of detachment, a feeling that while everyone else is moving forward, you are stuck in a loop of sleepless nights and exhausting shifts.

At the beginning, caffeine feels like a lifeline. A hot cup of coffee becomes your trusted companion, helping you fight off the overwhelming urge to sleep. It starts with one or two cups, then gradually increases as your body begins to rely on it just to function through the night. However, what initially seems like a solution soon turns into another problem. Too much caffeine comes with its own consequences. I remember reading a study during one of my "breaks" that highlighted the negative effects of excessive caffeine consumption. It disrupts your already fragile sleep patterns, making it even harder to get proper rest during the day. Instead of feeling refreshed after sleep, you wake up groggy, as if you never really rested at all. The side effects do not stop there—anxiety, digestive issues, increased heart rates, and mood swings become part of your daily life. It is ironic, really. The very thing you rely on to stay awake ultimately makes you feel worse.

The physical toll of night shifts is something few people talk about, but it is impossible to ignore. Working against the body's natural circadian rhythm takes more than just a mental toll—it has serious long-term health consequences. Studies have shown that those who work night shifts are at a higher risk of developing sleep disorders, cardiovascular diseases, obesity, and even depression. The human body is not designed to be awake all night and asleep all day, no matter how much you try to convince yourself otherwise. Fatigue becomes a constant companion, and no matter how much you sleep, you never feel truly rested. Your eating habits suffer as well—midnight snacks and unhealthy meals become the norm since regular, balanced meals are hard to maintain with such an erratic schedule. Exercise feels like an impossible task when all you want to do after a shift is collapse into bed.

And yet, despite the exhaustion, the stress, and the health risks, the demands of the job do not change. The chats keep coming, the targets keep increasing, and the pressure to maintain productivity remains relentless. There is little room for empathy or understanding—whether you are physically drained or emotionally exhausted, the expectation is the same: be present, be polite, and handle each chat as efficiently as possible. One of the hardest parts about working a night shift is that very few people truly understand what it is like. From the outside, it might seem like just another job with an unconventional schedule. But for those living it, it is a constant battle against exhaustion, loneliness, and deteriorating health. You see your coworkers going through the same struggles, yet it feels like no one is talking about it. It is an unspoken reality—something everyone experiences but rarely acknowledges.

At the end of the day (or night, in this case), you wonder: is it worth it? The paycheck, the stability, the routine—does it outweigh the cost of missing out on life? For some, the answer is yes. For others, the realization comes too late, when their health has already taken a hit. The world runs on daylight, and working against that natural rhythm comes at a price.

The shifts start every two hours like clockwork, and it feels less like an office and more like a massive production line, churning employees in and out with mechanical precision. You walk in, log into your system, and begin taking chats or calls, knowing that the moment your shift ends, another batch of agents will take your place, keeping the cycle running without pause. It is an endless loop, one that makes you feel more like a cog in an enormous, ever-turning machine rather than an individual with aspirations, emotions, and a life outside of work. There is no real sense of ownership, no feeling of contributing to something meaningful—just the monotonous repetition of interactions, solving the same problems for different people, with no time to stop and think about anything beyond the next chat in queue.

Sometimes, it feels as if you are less of an employee and more of a laborer, someone working tirelessly to keep the system functioning, unseen and undervalued. The irony of the situation does not escape you. As a customer support agent, your entire job revolves around helping people, resolving their issues, and making their lives easier. Yet, at the very moments when you are running on empty—when exhaustion creeps into your bones, when your mind begs for rest, when your body screams for relief—you find yourself craving the very thing you are expected to provide: support. Support from the management, who expect you to be available no matter how exhausted you are. Support from the system, which treats you like a replaceable unit rather than a human being. Support from anyone who understands what it feels like to push through the nights, pretending to be alert, pretending to be engaged, when all you really want to do is close your eyes and escape.

Yet somehow, life goes on. You adapt, or at least you convince yourself that you do. Night shifts are not just about staying awake—they are about enduring, about navigating a system that demands so much from you while giving back so little. You find small moments of solace—a shared joke with a colleague during a coffee break, the quiet camaraderie of knowing that the person next to you is going through the same struggle. There is a strange kind of comfort in that shared exhaustion, a mutual understanding that no words need to express. But even in those moments of laughter, even when you try to embrace the life you have been given, there is an undeniable truth lurking beneath it all: it is taking a toll. Because when the world is asleep and you are awake, it is hard not to feel like you are living a life that does not entirely belong to you.

You give everything you have to this job. You show up every night, put in your best effort, meet targets, follow the scripts, and maintain the company's standards. But at what cost? At the end of it all, you realize that the life you once had—the friendships, the family dinners, the weekend get-togethers—has started slipping away. You barely see your friends anymore because your schedules never align. Your conversations with relatives become short and infrequent, filled with rushed exchanges and empty reassurances of catching up "someday." The world outside feels distant, almost like a parallel universe that you can observe but not be a part of.

The isolation is not just physical; it is mental, emotional, and social. It does not matter which political party is making headlines, what social movements are gaining traction, or whether India is playing a crucial cricket match against Australia. Those things, which once sparked excitement and conversation, now feel irrelevant. Your reality has shrunk to the confines of your night shift routine, a bubble where time blurs and days lose meaning. The concept of weekends—a simple, universally understood break from work—becomes distorted.

During training, there was talk of a proper Saturday-Sunday weekend, a small but reassuring promise that at least some normalcy would remain intact. But that illusion quickly shatters once reality sets in. The traditional weekend vanishes, replaced by rotational shifts that seem to be assigned with little regard for how they impact your personal life. Suddenly, your "weekend" lands on a random Tuesday or Wednesday, days when the rest of the world is busy working. The first time it happens, you tell yourself it is just an adjustment period, that you will figure out a way to make it work. But as time goes on, you start to wonder—what exactly are you supposed to do on a weekday off, when all your friends and family are occupied with their own jobs?

It is a strange kind of loneliness, one that does not hit you all at once but slowly creeps in over time. At first, you do not notice it. You spend your days off catching up on sleep, watching shows, or scrolling mindlessly through your phone. But then, as the weeks turn into months, the emptiness becomes more apparent. No plans, no outings, no invitations to weekend gatherings—just the quiet realization that the world has moved on without you.

Your phone sits beside you, notifications popping up from group chats filled with messages you can never fully engage with. Friends make plans, but you are never available at the right time. You tell yourself you will catch up with them eventually, but eventually never seems to come. Instead, you spend your off days alone, scrolling endlessly through social media, watching other people live lives that seem so distant from your own. You think about messaging someone, about making an effort to reconnect, but what would you even say? That you have been too tired, too drained, too absent? That the job that was supposed to be just a career move has somehow taken over everything?

And so, you do nothing. You put your phone down, stare at the ceiling, and wonder how long this life is sustainable. You tell yourself it is just temporary, just a phase. But deep down, you know it is more than that. Because when the world is asleep, and you are awake, you are not just losing sleep—you are losing time, losing moments, losing pieces of yourself that you might never get back.

I still remember the way we had to fight tooth and nail just to get a single holiday approved. It was never a simple request; it always felt like a negotiation, like you were pleading for something that should have been a basic right. Even if you had a valid reason—be it a family wedding, a religious festival, or even a much-needed mental health break—the process was exhausting. It always felt like you were asking for a favor rather than claiming something you genuinely deserved. The management's favorite response was always the same, almost scripted: "We'll pay you extra if you work on national holidays." But what was the point? How could a few extra rupees ever replace the joy of sitting with your family during Diwali, of celebrating a loved one's birthday, or of simply having the chance to wake up without an alarm on a festive morning?

The idea that a small monetary incentive could compensate for missing out on life's important moments was frustrating. It wasn't about the money—it was about being present. About sharing laughter with family, catching up with friends over home-cooked meals, and feeling like you were a part of something beyond just your job. But in the world of night shifts and relentless schedules, those things started slipping away. Instead of looking forward to celebrations, we started dreading them, knowing we'd either be stuck at work or too exhausted to truly enjoy them.

And then there were the elections. Whenever election season came around, we knew what was coming. We'd hear the same line from management, instructing us to be available "for support." Support for what, exactly? Customers who would barely notice whether we were there or not? Calls and chats that had nothing to do with the elections, just the same mundane complaints we handled every day? Meanwhile, the very people we were assisting—those calling in to complain about their orders, demanding immediate solutions—were the ones actually enjoying their day off, living their lives, making plans, casting their votes, while we sat in a brightly lit office, pretending we weren't missing out on yet another moment that mattered.

Seasons didn't matter. Whether it was the peak of summer or the dead of winter, the struggle remained the same. Some agents had shifts that started at 2 a.m., which meant if you lived in a city like Delhi, your pick-up time was set at 1 a.m. That, in turn, meant waking up at midnight just to get ready for a shift that would leave you drained before the sun even rose. And the worst part? Even when the shift ended, your day wasn't over. The drop-off could take another one to two hours, depending on the route, the traffic, and how many stops had to be made.

So what was supposed to be a nine-hour shift often turned into a twelve-hour ordeal, if not longer. Time stopped making sense. You woke up at odd hours, traveled in the middle of the night, worked while the world was asleep, and returned home when the streets were just beginning to stir. The exhaustion became a permanent state, something you carried with you even on your days off. No amount of sleep seemed to be enough. No number of naps could make up for the disjointed, unnatural routine your body was forced into.

I've seen it in people's eyes—the weariness, the deep, dark circles forming under them, the way their tempers became short, their patience wore thin. Conversations became clipped, interactions robotic. Slowly, they started resembling ghosts of themselves, their personalities dulled by exhaustion, their minds too foggy to process anything beyond their immediate tasks. It wasn't just tiredness; it was a slow, relentless drain on their very being, a transformation into something that barely resembled a fully functioning human being.

There were days when it felt like we were all just walking through life in a haze, sleepwalking, running on autopilot with no real awareness of where we were or what time it was. The days and nights blurred together, merging into an indistinguishable cycle of work, travel, and restless sleep. It was almost surreal, like some kind of weird drug was coursing through our veins, numbing us to everything except the necessity of getting through the next shift.

Sometimes, you couldn't even tell if you were dreaming or if it was just another chat waiting in queue. It was a strange, unsettling feeling—the kind where reality and exhaustion intertwined so deeply that you no longer knew which one was which. I remember moments where I would close my eyes for just a second, only to jolt awake, wondering if I had actually dozed off or if my mind had just drifted away momentarily. Even when I slept, my body remained tense, my brain half-alert, as if it had been wired to expect the next ping of an incoming chat.

The worst part was, no one truly talked about it. It was just accepted as part of the job, as something we had to deal with, as if exhaustion was a badge of honor rather than a symptom of a system that demanded too much. And we carried on, night after night, shift after shift, hoping that at some point, life would feel normal again.

The shift timings? They were never truly fixed. One month, you'd find yourself working the graveyard shift, adjusting to the eerie quiet of a world that felt asleep while you struggled to stay alert. Just when you thought you had settled into that routine—mastering the art of forcing yourself to sleep in broad daylight, training your body to function when it was supposed to rest—everything would change. Suddenly, you'd be moved to the day shift, and your body, already confused, would be forced into another brutal adjustment. Then, before you could catch your breath, the morning shift would creep up on you, throwing your sleep schedule into absolute chaos again. No matter how much effort you put into adapting, it never really worked. Your body was constantly playing catch-up, always just a step behind, never fully rested, never truly at ease.

It felt like a cruel game—just when you thought you had found some semblance of stability, the schedule would change again, pulling the rug out from under you. There was no winning, no real way to balance life around a shifting work schedule that seemed to have no consideration for the people living through it. The exhaustion wasn't just physical—it was mental, emotional, the kind that seeped into your bones and settled in, becoming a part of you.

We were given breaks, of course—three short ones, 15 minutes each, making up a total of just 30 minutes in a shift that stretched across hours of relentless chats. But those breaks? They were barely enough. It wasn't like stepping away and taking a breath—it was more like pressing pause on an already overwhelming routine, knowing you'd be forced to hit play again in just a few minutes.

For some of us, though, there were small mercies. Thanks to Mohak, our team lead, and our floor coordinator, who we had a decent rapport with, we had the privilege of stretching our breaks just a little longer when we needed it. It was an unspoken understanding, a silent nod of recognition that sometimes, 15 minutes just wasn't enough to reset. But not everyone was that lucky. If your TL wasn't Mohak, you were stuck with the bare minimum. There was no leeway, no extra time, just the strict countdown of those 30 minutes spread thin over a long, draining shift.

And in those precious moments, we had to do everything—eat, drink, check our phones, catch up on the outside world, and maybe, if we were lucky, take a quick walk to clear our heads. It felt like life was permanently in fast-forward mode. There was no leisurely meal, no relaxed scrolling through messages, no time to breathe and feel human again. You shoved food down quickly, skimmed through unread texts, and in the briefest of moments, tried to remind yourself that there was a world outside of work. But it never lasted long.

The second that break ended, it was like snapping back into reality. The illusion of freedom vanished, and you were back at your desk, back to the same grind, staring at the same screen, engaging in the same routine. The same tired eyes, the same never-ending cycle, the same slow drain of energy that no amount of caffeine or forced optimism could fix. Those breaks weren't really breaks—they were just temporary illusions, fleeting moments where you tricked yourself into believing that you still had a life beyond the four walls of the office. But deep down, you knew it wasn't enough. It was never enough.

It felt like we were nothing more than punching bags, standing on the front lines, taking every hit—verbal, emotional, sometimes even personal. No matter how unfair the complaints were, no matter how unreasonable the demands, we had to absorb it all, keep our cool, and respond with a scripted politeness that felt more exhausting than the work itself. The worst part? Most of the time, we didn't even have the solutions the customers were looking for.

We lacked access to the right tools, the crucial information, and—most frustratingly—the authority to actually fix the problem. We were the voice of the company, the ones bearing the brunt of customers' anger, but without the power to truly resolve their issues. Instead, we had to improvise, find ways to calm them down, apologize for things completely out of our control, and, somehow, in the middle of all that, attempt to upsell products or services. It was like being asked to repair a car without tools and then still expected to convince the owner to buy an upgrade.

And the customers? They didn't get it. Or maybe they did, but they didn't care. To them, we weren't individuals—we were just faceless representatives of the company, the only ones they could yell at when things went wrong. They didn't know—or maybe didn't want to know—that we were just following policies, restricted by decisions made far above our pay grade. There was no room to explain that we were just doing our jobs. We couldn't say what we really thought, because that would be the end of it. Instead, we had to keep the act going—smiling, apologizing, making polite conversation while enduring insults that left invisible bruises.

Because that was the job. No matter how much we wanted to push back, no one would listen. Complaining wouldn't change anything. There was no sympathy for the people behind the screen, no real acknowledgment that we, too, were human. It was as if we were invisible, mere voices trapped inside an endless system of chats, responding to wave after wave of frustration, anger, and impossible expectations. And when the shift finally ended, we weren't left with a sense of accomplishment—just the echoes of every insult, every unreasonable demand, every moment where we had to suppress our own emotions just to get through another conversation.

Before every shift, the same thought ran through our minds: This is it. I can't do this anymore. We told ourselves that we'd find a way out, that we'd study something new, build new skills, and escape this cycle. The idea of leaving, of stepping into a world where we weren't reduced to a headset and a set of templated responses, seemed like the only thing keeping us going. We even started making mental checklists—certifications we needed, courses we should take, industries we could transition into.

But as soon as the shift ended, exhaustion would crash over us like a relentless tide, sweeping away any remaining energy we had left. It wasn't just physical fatigue; it was mental and emotional too, the kind that seeped into our bones and made even the simplest tasks feel impossible. The moment we logged out, our bodies seemed to finally acknowledge just how drained we were, as if they had been holding on to the last shreds of strength just to make it through.

The idea of opening a book, updating a résumé, or researching a new career path—things we had promised ourselves we would do—felt like climbing a mountain with no strength left in our limbs. We would collapse into our beds, eyes heavy, whispering the same promise we made everytime: Tomorrow, I'll start fresh. Tomorrow, I'll take the first step toward something better. But when tomorrow came, the cycle reset itself. The alarm would blare, we would drag ourselves out of bed, force down some food, and step back into the same chair, staring at the same screens, preparing for another long shift.

That ambition, that dream of escaping, slowly dulled with each passing day. It was like being trapped in quicksand—the more we thought about breaking free, the heavier the weight on our shoulders became, sinking us deeper into the routine. The cruel irony of it all was that we desperately wanted change, but we were too exhausted to fight for it.

Yet, despite everything, not every moment in the BPO was bleak. If there was one saving grace, one thing that kept us going, it was our team. We weren't just coworkers; we were survivors of the same relentless grind, bound together by shared struggles and inside jokes that only we would understand. Between endless chats, ticket resolutions, and customer escalations, we found ways to lighten the mood. We cracked jokes over Slack, turned frustrating customers into amusing anecdotes, and even had little competitions about who could handle the most difficult complaint with the coolest composure. These moments, however small, were our sanity.

But let me tell you, there was always someone who seemed to have a personal vendetta against our happiness. If we laughed a little too loudly, even for a moment, we would be met with piercing glares from senior managers sitting just a few desks away. Their expressions were always the same—disapproving, irritated, as if our laughter was an act of rebellion. How dare you enjoy yourselves?

It wasn't just laughter that was frowned upon. Even something as basic as standing up to stretch or taking a sip of water at the wrong moment could draw unnecessary scrutiny. It was as if they believed that if we weren't constantly glued to our screens, hammering away at our keyboards, then we weren't doing our jobs. Productivity wasn't measured by how well we solved customer issues; it was measured by how robotic we could become.

There were days when we would look at each other and ask, Are we actually working, or are we just prisoners to this chair and these two monitors? The lines blurred so much that it became difficult to tell whether we were doing meaningful work or just serving as living, breathing cogs in a machine designed to function at maximum efficiency. Our job wasn't just about answering queries—it was about learning how to keep our spirits alive in an environment that seemed determined to crush them.

And then there was the calling department—a whole different battlefield. If we thought our work was tough, theirs was an all-out war. I remember a conversation I had with Neha from the calls team during one of our breaks. She looked exhausted, her face carrying the weight of back-to-back calls with no respite.

"Customers don't even let you mute or pause for a second," she sighed, rubbing her temples. "They want an answer, and they want it now. If you don't give them what they want immediately, they either start yelling or hang up, only to call back even angrier."

I could see the toll it had taken on her—not just the constant demands of impatient customers but also the pressure from within. Her manager, instead of supporting her, was known for his public call-outs. No matter how many calls she handled flawlessly, no matter how many customer issues she resolved, it was never acknowledged. But the moment she made a mistake—one tiny error, one call that didn't go as planned—it was a public spectacle.

She shook her head, her voice tired but resigned. "At least in chats, you guys can type out your frustrations or take a breather while the customer replies. Here, I don't even get that luxury. It's just nonstop."

Listening to her made me realize that no one in this industry had it easy. Every agent, whether handling chats or calls, had their own version of the same exhausting grind. We all suffered in different ways—ours in silence, hers in the loud chaos of a call.

And yet, despite it all, we kept showing up. Shift after shift, day after day, we put on our headsets, adjusted our chairs, and braced ourselves for another round. We found strength in each other, in shared jokes, in fleeting moments of laughter, in the silent understanding of what it meant to be in this together.

Somehow, we survived another shift. Somehow, we made it through. And maybe, just maybe, that was enough—at least for now.

You probably have a question—Why don't they just leave the job? Why not break free from this never-ending cycle of exhaustion and monotony?

The truth is, it's never that simple. There's always something that keeps you hooked, something that convinces you that staying just a little longer won't hurt. Maybe it's the steady paycheck, the comfort of knowing what to expect, even if what you expect is exhaustion. Or maybe, it's the little luxuries that make the struggle feel worthwhile—the new phone on EMI, the wireless earbuds you've been eyeing, the occasional weekend splurge that makes you feel like all this work is leading somewhere.

It's ironic, really. The very things meant to make life enjoyable—gadgets, clothes, short-lived indulgences—end up chaining you to the same routine. Because as soon as the bills come in, as soon as the EMI reminders start flashing on your phone, you realize you can't just walk away. You tell yourself, Just one more month. I'll save a little more. I'll clear my dues. Then I'll leave. But the cycle keeps pulling you back in. Another festival, another upgrade, another reason to stay just a little longer.

And so, shift after shift, month after month, we follow the same schedule, convincing ourselves that we'll leave soon. But soon never comes.

SEVEN

The Pressure Cooker

Another day was passing, just like all the others, in the endless loop of the day and night shift. The floor was always full of bad moods—a mix of frustration, exhaustion, and silent resentment hanging in the air like a fog that never lifted. People moved mechanically, heads down, fingers tapping away at keyboards, their faces illuminated by the glow of monitors. Conversations were minimal, just enough to function—nothing more.

For most teams, the standard greeting was still there. A casual "Hi" or "Hello" exchanged in passing, a weak attempt at normalcy. But for us? We didn't bother anymore. What was the point? We had long stopped pretending that any of this was okay. Our version of small talk had been reduced to a glance, a nod, or, at best, a muttered "Start your shift already." The office had become a revolving door of new faces and old ones fading away. Fresh batches of recruits arrived every few months, their enthusiasm shining brightly—at least in the beginning. For us, though, life had shrunk to a single repetitive cycle: "Hi," "Hello," "Work," "Go home." The world outside had stopped mattering.

Despite the monotony, our team had somehow managed to keep the atmosphere lively. No single person was responsible for the humor and camaraderie—it was a collective effort. Everyone brought their own quirks to the table. There was Saloni, the sharp-witted one; Mohak, the unyielding yet supportive TL; Karan, Anshuman, Sahil, Vishal, Anjali, Prabhat, and even me—each of us had our role. Jassi and Netai? They could turn even the dullest moments into fits of laughter. It was as if we'd all taken a silent oath to inject some fun into the suffocating routine.

For a while, life felt manageable, even in the ups and downs of the night shift. But then came the shift that turned everything upside down. Manish Sir left.

He had been the one thing holding everything together—not because he made the job easy, but because he at least understood. He wasn't the type to breathe down our necks over numbers or demand impossible targets. If something went wrong, he backed us up. If someone was struggling, he noticed. He knew how to push us without making us feel like we were just numbers on a performance sheet.

But one day, just like that, he was gone. Transferred to another process without warning, without any chance to adjust. No explanations. No goodbyes. Just a sudden absence that hit harder than any of us expected.

In his place came Gaurav, someone entirely new. Almost overnight, the dynamics began to change. The other TLs quickly aligned themselves with Gaurav, eager to win his favor. But Mohak? He was different. He had never been one to bow down or say "yes" just to please someone. And for that, he stayed on the outside.

What none of us realized was how dangerous the consequences of this shift would be. The small, silent cracks in our routine and team spirit were about to widen into something far more destructive.

Rumors began to swirl around the floor, whispered between chats, passed along in hushed tones during breaks. The client wasn't happy with our performance. Or maybe, as some of us joked bitterly, the client had simply lost their mind. No one knew the full story, but the tension in the air was undeniable. It started with small, subtle changes—requests for extra reports, sudden increases in quality audits, a sharper tone from management. Then came the first real blow that no one had expected.

Without any prior warning, overtime was removed. Just like that, the extra hours that many had relied on to make ends meet were gone. It wasn't just about the money, though for some, like Prabhat, losing that additional income meant serious financial strain. It was about the principle of it—about taking away one of the few things that made the grind feel worthwhile. Before this, at least those who wanted to push through the exhaustion could do so for some extra pay. Now, we were expected to deliver the same energy and output without any additional reward. It felt like yet another way to drain us dry.

But that wasn't the only thing that changed. Sales targets, which were already difficult, suddenly became even more extreme. The numbers we were expected to hit seemed impossible, almost like they had been pulled out of thin air by someone who had never actually done the job. Management wouldn't hear any complaints; they didn't care about the challenges we faced, the customers who weren't interested, or the sheer saturation of the market. All they wanted were results. "Find a way," they'd say, as if it were that simple. Every meeting, every email, every pep talk boiled down to the same message—push harder, sell more, and don't bring excuses.

New processes and rules were introduced overnight, confusing everyone. What was fine yesterday was suddenly unacceptable today. Quality audits became stricter, scripting guidelines became suffocating, and every chat or call was monitored with even more scrutiny. There was no room for flexibility anymore. Even the most skilled agents started struggling under the weight of these new expectations. It felt like we weren't just working; we were constantly being tested, judged, and prepared for failure.

It wasn't long before desperation started creeping in. The pressure was unbearable, and some people cracked under it. That's when the fake sales started. At first, it was just a whisper—something that only a handful of people knew about. A few agents, unable to meet the impossible targets, had begun logging false transactions. Some found loopholes in the system, others faked customer confirmations. It was risky, but for a short while, it worked. Numbers went up, and those who faked their way through actually ended up being praised by management.

But nothing stays hidden for long. Once the fraud was discovered, everything changed. Every single sale was now questioned. Legitimate deals were held up for additional verification, agents had to fight to prove their work was real, and the entire floor was suddenly under suspicion. Those who had never even considered bending the rules were treated the same as those who had taken advantage of the system. It didn't matter if you were honest or not—the company no longer trusted any of us.

The job had always been exhausting, but now it felt suffocating. The floor was no longer just a workplace; it was a battlefield. Every shift became a test of endurance, a fight to stay afloat in a system that seemed designed to crush us. And the worst part was, no one knew what was coming next.

But there was another unspoken rule in this toxic system: if you shone too brightly, people began to notice—and not always in a good way. It didn't matter how skilled you were, how hard you worked, or how much your team admired you. Standing out could be dangerous, and no one learned that lesson faster than Mohak.

As a TL, Mohak wasn't just a leader—he was the kind of person people actually wanted to follow. He was fair, approachable, and always had his team's back. If there was an issue, he handled it. If someone was struggling, he made sure they got the support they needed. Unlike other TLs who focused solely on numbers, Mohak understood that behind every metric was a person, and that made all the difference. Under his guidance, our team had thrived. We weren't just performing well; we were one of the best teams on the floor.

But that was before Gaurav arrived.

The moment Gaurav took over as the new manager, everything started to change. At first, it was subtle—an occasional remark here, a slight shift in tone there. But soon, it became clear that he had set his sights on Mohak. Maybe it was because he didn't like how much the team respected him. Maybe it was because Mohak refused to blindly obey without questioning orders. Or maybe it was just the way the corporate world worked: anyone who didn't bow down was seen as a threat.

Whatever the reason, Gaurav made sure Mohak knew his place.

The tension on the floor was impossible to ignore. Conversations that once flowed easily were now cut short. Laughter that once echoed across the room had turned into uneasy silence. It felt like we were all walking on eggshells, waiting for the next storm to hit. And then, the numbers started slipping.

At first, it was barely noticeable—just a small dip here and there. But soon, the decline became impossible to ignore. The team that had once ranked at the top was now struggling at the bottom. Targets were missed. Performance scores dropped. Complaints increased. And no one could understand why.

I've never been one to believe in luck or superstition, but this felt like something beyond logic. The agents were the same. The customers were the same. The job itself hadn't changed. So how was it possible that what we were doing right yesterday had suddenly become wrong today?

It was as if something invisible had infected the team—a slow, creeping force that drained our energy, our motivation, and our will to fight back. Maybe it was the constant pressure. Maybe it was the fear of being singled out, just like Mohak. Or maybe it was the realization that no matter how hard we worked, it would never be enough.

And yet, we kept showing up. Day after day, shift after shift, hoping—foolishly—that things might somehow go back to the way they were. But deep down, we all knew the truth. The workplace had become a battlefield, and Mohak, once a celebrated leader, was now caught in the crossfire. And if someone like him could be taken down, what chance did the rest of us have?

That's the brutal reality of working in a BPO. No matter how well you perform, recognition is never guaranteed. You could spend months exceeding expectations, meeting impossible targets, and pulling off what seemed like miracles in customer service, but it wouldn't matter. Because praise in this industry was like a passing breeze—fleeting, barely noticeable, and gone before you could even acknowledge it.

But make one mistake? That mistake became your identity. It didn't matter how many flawless shifts you'd worked before. The moment you slipped up, it was like a stain that wouldn't wash off. You'd hear about it in every meeting, see it reflected in your performance reports, and be reminded of it through every passive-aggressive email from management. And while success was treated as just part of the job, failure was turned into a spectacle—dissected, magnified, and held against you for weeks, sometimes months.

For the longest time, we had believed Mohak was untouchable. He had always been solid—so reliable that even other managers respected him, trusting him with responsibilities most TLs couldn't handle. Under his leadership, our team had thrived. If Mohak was at the helm, success followed. It wasn't luck; it was the way he led. He knew how to bring out the best in his team without breaking them in the process.

But then Gaurav arrived, and everything changed.

We had never seen Mohak get reprimanded before. Sure, there were days when targets weren't met, but it was never because of a lack of effort. He always had valid reasons, and the previous management had understood that. But this time was different. This time, it wasn't about logic or performance—it was about control. Gaurav needed to establish his dominance, and Mohak, with his independent thinking and team loyalty, was standing in the way.

It was strange, watching him stand there, taking the verbal blows from someone who had only been around for a few weeks. It wasn't just unfair; it was unsettling. The same Mohak who had once been a pillar of strength now looked cornered, and there was nothing any of us could do about it.

And then, the cracks spread even further.

Vishal and Anshuman, two of the most skilled sales agents on the floor, were no longer the confident, sharp-tongued closers we had always known. Their energy was gone, drained out of them by the mounting pressure and impossible targets. They still tried, of course—they were fighters, after all. But there was something different in their eyes now. A kind of exhaustion that went beyond just a bad shift or a rough customer. It was the look of people who had been pushed too far, for too long, with no end in sight.

And if even they were struggling—agents who had spent years mastering the art of persuasion, of turning hesitant customers into guaranteed sales—what did that mean for the rest of us?

The customers weren't making things any easier. They came in angry, frustrated with their own issues, and took it all out on us. It didn't matter that we were just there to help. It didn't matter that we were following the very policies their own companies had put in place. All they saw were faceless agents, and all they cared about was venting their rage.

We would do our best to pacify them, to offer solutions, to fix their problems—but some people didn't want solutions. They wanted someone to blame. And once they got what they wanted—once they had screamed, insulted, and drained every last bit of patience from us—they would leave. And with them, they would take the only thing that mattered in this job: our ratings.

A single bad rating could undo an entire week of effort. It didn't matter how good you had been to the last ten customers; the one who decided to leave you with a perfect 0 was the one who defined your performance.

It was a vicious cycle. A downward spiral that none of us could escape. We were drowning, and no one—not management, not the clients, and certainly not the customers—seemed to care. And so, we just kept falling, waiting to hit a bottom that never seemed to come.

The new manager had a way of making his presence felt—like a mosquito buzzing in your ear at 2 AM, impossible to ignore and thoroughly irritating. He didn't just observe from a distance like a normal person or give constructive feedback in meetings. No, that would have been way too reasonable. Instead, he lurked around the floor like some corporate ghost, materializing behind you just as you were about to take a sip of coffee or breathe for the first time in an hour.

His favorite pastime? Hovering over our shoulders like a vulture waiting for its prey to mess up. His sharp eyes scanned our screens with the intensity of a detective solving a high-stakes crime, except the crime was something as petty as a typo in an email or a slight delay in response time. His voice, colder than the AC that was always set too high, cut through the office air like a knife.

"Is that how you talk to a customer?" Cue the entire floor going silent.

Mistakes weren't just pointed out—they were broadcasted, dissected, and turned into full-fledged horror shows for everyone to witness. He thrived on intimidation, wielding power like a toddler who just discovered the volume button on a toy megaphone. Fear wasn't just a side effect of his leadership style—it was the main event. If stress burned calories, we'd all be runway models by now.

Every time he approached, we collectively held our breath, pretending to be deeply engrossed in our screens while secretly praying he would pick another victim. But no one was safe. He had an uncanny ability to show up exactly when you least expected it—like a jumpscare in a horror movie, except instead of a ghost, it was a middle-aged man in a wrinkled dress shirt with a Bluetooth headset he clearly didn't need.

And just when you thought he was gone? Boom. There he was again, arms crossed, eyes squinted, waiting to strike with another round of soul-crushing "feedback."

Honestly, if there were an Olympic sport for making employees miserable, he'd be bringing home the gold.

Under the previous manager, things had been different—almost like living in an entirely different universe where employees weren't treated like malfunctioning robots but as actual human beings. Manish Sir had a rare quality in leadership: balance. He knew how to push us toward excellence without shoving us off a cliff in the process. He wasn't the kind of boss who relied on fear to get results. No ominous lurking, no dramatic callouts in front of the entire team, and definitely no soul-crushing monologues about how disappointed he was.

Instead, he led with a mix of encouragement and accountability. If you messed up, he didn't launch into an investigation like you had just committed corporate treason. He'd call you aside, explain the issue, and actually help you fix it. The way he handled feedback made all the difference—he didn't treat mistakes like personal failures but as learning opportunities. He had this way of making you want to improve, not because you were terrified of him, but because you respected him.

And that respect? It was mutual. He understood that we weren't machines designed to endlessly churn out results without feeling exhausted. He knew when to push and when to ease up, like a coach who recognized that peak performance required rest, motivation, and trust. It was this very approach that made us work harder—not out of obligation, but out of genuine willingness.

Under his leadership, there was a sense of purpose. We believed in what we were doing because he made sure we understood why it mattered. He didn't just bark orders and expect miracles; he gave us clarity, guidance, and the autonomy to make decisions. He had expectations, sure, but they were reasonable. He wanted us to succeed—not so he could brag about numbers in meetings, but because he genuinely cared about our growth.

And perhaps that was why, during his time, our scores had been consistently high. Not because we were forced to comply under the looming threat of punishment, but because we felt valued. Because we wanted to succeed. Because, for once, we weren't just another cog in the machine—we were a team.

But now, that belief was gone. The pressure wasn't just mounting—it was suffocating. Every shift felt like walking into a warzone where the enemy wasn't an opposing force but the very people who were supposed to lead us. Expectations were drilled into us like battle cries: perform, sell, meet your targets—or else. And that unspoken 'or else' was a constant, looming threat. It was there in Gaurav's sharp tone, in the coldness of his emails, in the way our once-supportive TLs could no longer afford to stand up for us. The work environment became toxic, a place where fear and stress festered like an open wound.

It was no surprise that our scores began to plummet. How could we perform well when we were constantly on edge, walking on eggshells, waiting for the next round of scolding? How could we focus on selling when our minds were consumed with thoughts of avoiding yet another public humiliation? The customers could sense it too. They weren't oblivious to the exhaustion in our voices, the forced enthusiasm that barely masked our dread. And when customers sensed an agent didn't care, they, in turn, stopped caring. They grew ruder, more impatient. They lashed out at us, their words cutting like knives, their ratings dropping lower and lower. Our mental health suffered, our motivation dwindled, and our performance spiraled further downward.

The sales weren't just declining—they were collapsing. And with every passing day, the atmosphere in the office grew heavier, pressing down on us like an unbearable weight. What had once been a simple job, a way to make a living, now felt like a punishment. The sense of camaraderie that had kept us going through the hardest of days had evaporated. Breaks, which were once moments of respite, were now barely long enough to catch our breath. Conversations over coffee turned into silent stares at vending machines, and laughter was replaced with whispered escape plans—courses to take, companies to apply to, the idea of quitting without a backup plan becoming more tempting with each passing shift.

Even Mohak, our once steadfast leader, was beginning to crack under the pressure. He had always been the one to shield us, to absorb the blows so that we wouldn't have to. But how much could one person take before breaking? Every day, he and Diljit (SME) were called to the board where the team scores were displayed like marks of failure for all to see. The reprimands that followed were swift and merciless, a reminder that no matter how hard we tried, it would never be enough.

Mohak bore it all in silence, but the weight of it trickled down to us. He was no longer the cheerful, easygoing leader we had once known. The person who had once turned our jokes into laughter now snapped at the smallest quip. The warmth of 'Mohak bro' had been replaced with the cold formality of 'Mohak sir.' The shift was undeniable, and it affected us all. Our team began to feel like a pressure cooker—agents boiling under stress, with no release, no escape. The fear of stepping into the office clung to us like a shadow we couldn't shake. Some of us began experiencing anxiety attacks; others withdrew completely, reduced to mere shells of their former selves.

Then, it happened. The moment that shattered everything. The moment that proved, once again, why I should have listened to my own advice: Never make your colleagues or TL your friend.

Mohak and I, who had once been inseparable—who had shared countless inside jokes, lunch breaks, and late-night venting sessions about this hellhole—found ourselves standing on opposite sides of a battle that neither of us had even signed up for. The pressure had been mounting for weeks, suffocating us all like an invisible noose tightening around our throats. And finally, in one ugly, irreversible moment, it snapped.

We were mid-shift, buried under an avalanche of chat requests, the notification pings blurring into one endless, maddening sound. The floor buzzed with the usual undertones of exhaustion, frustration, and thinly-veiled resentment. It was just another miserable day in the corporate trenches—until Gaurav decided to unleash his usual tirade.

This time, his chosen target was Mohak. Again.

"Look at these numbers!" he barked, slamming his hand on the board as if it were our fault that customers were more interested in screaming at us than actually buying anything. "This is unacceptable. You're supposed to be leading this team, Mohak, not babysitting them!"

I watched as Mohak's expression tightened. He was reaching his limit—I could see it in the way his hands clenched into fists at his sides, the way his jaw tensed like he was physically holding back every unprofessional response bubbling under the surface.

And then, the mistake happened.

I don't even remember how it started. Maybe it was a snide remark. Maybe it was the way he looked at me—like I was just another part of the problem. Maybe it was the stress, the exhaustion, the unspoken resentment that had been festering for weeks. Whatever it was, it set off a chain reaction that neither of us could stop.

"You think I'm not trying?" Mohak's voice cracked under the weight of frustration. "Do you have any idea what I'm dealing with?"

And that was it. That was the moment I lost it.

"Oh, and you think it's just you under pressure?" I shot back, my voice sharper than I intended. "You think the rest of us are just coasting through this? That we don't feel the same weight crushing us every damn day?"

The words hung in the air like a live wire, sparking tension in every direction. Around us, heads turned. Eyes widened. The office, usually a chaotic blend of ringing phones and muffled customer complaints, had fallen deathly silent. No one dared to intervene. No one could.

Because this wasn't just a fight between two colleagues.

This was the eruption of everything we had been forced to swallow. Every unrealistic expectation. Every ignored complaint. Every moment of frustration that had been pushed down, disguised as "resilience."

We weren't really mad at each other.

We were mad at them. At the system that had turned us into enemies instead of allies. At the job that had drained every ounce of joy from our lives and left behind nothing but exhaustion and resentment.

But at that moment, none of that mattered. Because words had already been spoken. Damage had already been done.

When it was over, we sat in silence, both of us too stunned to move. I wanted to take it back. I wanted to tell him that I didn't mean it, that this wasn't his fault any more than it was mine.

But I couldn't.

Because no matter how much I wanted to believe our friendship was stronger than this job, the truth was clear: The job had already won.

Mohak looked at me, his eyes filled with something I couldn't quite decipher—defeat, exhaustion, regret. And in that moment, I realized something else:

This wasn't just about us.

This was about survival.

And I had just realized—I wasn't willing to fight anymore.

That was the moment I knew—I couldn't do this anymore.

Karan, my closest ally, my go-to person for venting sessions and inside jokes, chose to stand with Mohak.

I don't know why I expected anything different. Maybe it was my misplaced belief that our bond was unbreakable, that we had both suffered enough under this toxic system to understand each other. Maybe I thought he'd see things from my perspective—that he'd recognize that I wasn't the enemy, that the real problem was the relentless pressure and the suffocating work environment that had turned us against each other.

But instead, he made his choice.

And just like that, another crack formed in the foundation of what had once been a solid, unshakable friendship.

That was the moment it hit me like a punch to the gut—I was truly alone.

This job had taken everything. My peace of mind. My motivation. And now, the people I once called friends.

I sat at my desk, staring blankly at the screen as the chat notifications kept rolling in, the endless stream of complaints and unrealistic demands from customers a constant reminder of how meaningless this job had become. My fingers hovered over the keyboard, but I couldn't bring myself to type a response.

Because what was the point?

I had given everything to this job, and in return, it had drained me dry. No matter how much effort I put in, no matter how many targets I met, no matter how many extra hours I worked—it was never enough. And it never would be.

So, I made my decision.

I submitted my resignation.

It wasn't easy. Not because I doubted my choice, but because of how much of myself I had already lost to this place. It felt like leaving behind a part of me—one that had fought, struggled, and endured. But at the same time, it felt like reclaiming something even more important: myself.

And I wasn't the only one who felt this way.

One by one, my colleagues followed. Those who had once laughed during breaks, who had shared stories about their families, who had turned mundane workdays into something bearable—they were all slipping away. The team that had once felt like a family was now crumbling like a house of cards.

The laughter that once echoed in the breakroom? Gone.

The shared grumbles over impossible targets? Silenced.

The camaraderie that had kept us afloat in the worst of times? Shattered beyond repair.

All that remained was the unbearable weight of what this place had done to us.

So when I handed in my resignation, I was already prepared for what came next.

The inevitable.

The manager summoned me to his office, his face carefully composed, an expression of forced concern plastered across his features. He gestured for me to sit, as if we were about to have a heartfelt discussion—one where he would miraculously make me change my mind.

I humored him, lowering myself into the chair, my resignation letter still clutched in my hands.

And then, he leaned forward, hands folded, voice dripping with feigned sympathy.

"Why are you resigning?"

Ah, there it was—the predictable opening act. But before I could even think about responding, he launched into what I could only describe as a monologue worthy of an Oscar.

He talked about resilience. About loyalty. About how challenges make us stronger.

He painted himself as the protagonist of his own heroic story—a man who had faced hardships, persevered, and thrived.

I sat there, nodding politely, maintaining the perfect balance between attentive and indifferent. But inside? My thoughts were practically screaming.

You're the reason I'm doing this.

You're the reason my team fell apart.

You're the reason I dread coming here every single day.

I wanted to say it out loud. I wanted to throw the truth in his face. But I knew it wouldn't matter. People like him—people who thrived on control, who wielded authority like a weapon—never saw themselves as the problem.

And honestly? I didn't owe him an explanation.

When he finally finished his grand speech, he leaned back, waiting for me to reconsider, as if his words had somehow ignited a newfound sense of dedication in me.

But my mind was already made up.

I stood up, resignation letter still firm in my grip, and met his gaze with unwavering certainty.

"Thank you for sharing," I said, my voice steady. "But this is something I need to do."

I placed the letter on his desk, turned around, and walked out of that office with a sense of clarity I hadn't felt in months.

It wasn't just a resignation.

It was my escape.

And for the first time in what felt like forever, I could finally breathe.

I was free.

And there was no turning back.

EIGHT

ONE LAST LOGIN

Ask any corporate worker what the best feeling in the world is. No, it's not love. Not a vacation. Not even that first sip of chai in the morning. It's the resignation period—those final days at work when you are still technically employed but mentally already retired. The air feels lighter, the keyboard sounds softer, and suddenly, every task comes with a newfound sense of detachment.

For months—years, even—I had lived like a corporate puppet, responding to chat messages like my life depended on it. One delayed reply, and my manager would appear like a ghost in my inbox. "Why was this response late?" he'd ask, as if I hadn't just handled fifty chats simultaneously with the efficiency of a human chatbot. If I paused for even a minute, I'd get a suspicious "Are you facing any system issues?" No, sir, just facing life issues.

But then, everything changed. The moment my resignation was in, I was no longer trapped in the toxic corporate cycle. No. I became the toxin.

The transformation was almost immediate. I no longer flinched at the sound of incoming chat notifications. Where I once panicked over response time, I now stared at chats with the detached calm of a retired monk. "Oh, your refund is late? Tragic." My fingers, once trained for lightning-speed typing, now moved at the leisurely pace of someone who simply did not care. My manager, sensing my newfound apathy, tried to keep me in check. "We still need your support until your last working day," he reminded me. Oh, of course! He needn't have worried—I was physically present. Mentally, I was already on a beach, sipping coconut water.

And then came the best part—sharing my corporate survival wisdom with the fresh-faced new joiners who still believed in things like "growth" and "opportunities." I took it upon myself to prepare them for reality. "Oh, you think the 'open-door policy' means they listen? That's adorable." "You're working overtime to impress the manager? Don't bother—he barely remembers our names." "Excited about the office party? Hope you enjoy plain samosas and warm Coke." I was no longer training them to excel. I was training them to survive.

Every day brought new opportunities to test the limits of my notice-period freedom. I became an expert in late login and early logout. My new work motto? "I'm on my notice period—what more do you want from me?" I even invented a fun little game called How long can I ignore this email before my manager physically walks over to my desk? Turns out, the answer was two hours. When he finally did appear, looking at me like I had committed some unforgivable crime, I just blinked innocently. "Oh, I was just about to reply." Was I? Absolutely not.

And of course, what's a resignation period without a little mischief? My small acts of rebellion started harmlessly—forgetting minor tasks here and there, suddenly becoming "unavailable" for extra shifts. But then I took it up a notch. One day, I showed up with a bottle filled not with water—but with mango juice. My manager, eyeing me suspiciously, asked, "Why is your bottle full of juice?" I took a slow, dramatic sip and said, "Corporate survival technique."

Meetings? Skipped. Team engagement activities? Ignored. Every now and then, I'd turn my chair dramatically towards my teammates, sigh deeply, and say something wise like, "This company will never change." Did it help anyone? Probably not. Did it make me feel powerful? Absolutely.

Looking back, I sometimes wonder—was I always this chaotic? Or did the toxic workplace turn me into a toxic employee? Either way, my transformation was complete. I had become the Final Boss of the Resignation Period—a legend among notice-period employees, the hero every overworked worker secretly wanted to be.

And you know what? I was enjoying every second of it.

On the other hand, Anshuman and Vishal were also serving their notice periods, and together, we stood like battle-worn comrades walking away from the wreckage of a long and exhausting war. There was an unspoken bond between us now—a shared sense of freedom, a silent agreement that we had endured enough and were finally breaking free. Every day, we exchanged knowing glances, the kind that said, Just a little longer, and we're out of here. The final days felt less like work and more like a countdown to our collective escape.

However, not everyone saw it that way. Mohak, once a close friend and ally in the struggle, had grown distant. It was as if he had drawn a line between us, as if we had somehow betrayed the company by choosing to leave. His conversations with us became less frequent, his usual jokes replaced by curt responses and occasional cold stares. And then, as if searching for an explanation that didn't involve facing the truth, he convinced himself that I was the reason Anshuman and Vishal had decided to resign. To him, I had planted the idea in their heads, whispered words of rebellion, and led them down this path.

Perhaps he genuinely believed it. Or perhaps it was easier for him to blame me than to acknowledge the real reason behind the mass exits. Because deep down, he knew the truth—it wasn't me. It was the endless grind, the suffocating micromanagement, the lack of appreciation, the exhaustion of working for a system that treated us like disposable resources. The company didn't care about us. The moment one employee walked out, another took their place, like an assembly line of fresh hires doomed to the same cycle of overwork and underappreciation.

But maybe Mohak didn't want to see that. Maybe it was easier to believe that I had poisoned their minds than to admit that the company itself was the toxin. Maybe he feared that if he let himself think about it too much, he'd realize he was just as trapped as we had been. And maybe, just maybe, he wasn't ready to face the fact that one day, he would leave too.

After all, what reason was left to stay? There was no real motivation, no sense of purpose—just an endless cycle of draining shifts, robotic replies, and the constant feeling of being overworked and undervalued. The money? It had long since lost its appeal. Whatever paycheck we received barely justified the mental exhaustion, the unrealistic expectations, and the way our time was swallowed up by a job that gave nothing back. The workload? It had become a monster of its own, growing heavier with each passing day, crushing whatever energy or enthusiasm we once had.

In that BPO office, some agents like Prabhat and Anjali weren't just handling customer chats—they were carrying the weight of entire households on their shoulders. While most employees grumbled about long shifts and difficult customers, for them, this job was not just about earning a paycheck. It was about survival.

At just 21 and 22, they had become the unsung heroes of their families, stepping into responsibilities that most people their age couldn't even fathom. While their peers spent their evenings debating which Netflix series to binge or scrolling through social media without a care, Prabhat and Anjali sat in their dimly lit workstations, fingers flying across the keyboard, typing out polite responses to an endless stream of complaints, queries, and demands. Their customers remained faceless, their struggles unseen. No one on the other side of the chat window knew what it took for them to show up every day, to smile through the exhaustion, to keep going despite everything.

Prabhat's story was one of quiet resilience. He didn't just juggle multiple chat windows—he juggled the survival of his entire family. Life had been relatively normal until a year ago when his father, the family's sole breadwinner, suddenly fell ill. At first, they had hoped it was something minor, something that would pass. But as days turned into weeks and doctor visits turned into hospital stays, reality hit them hard. His father wasn't getting better, and with every new prescription, every test, every medical bill, their savings vanished like water slipping through their fingers.

The bills didn't wait. The landlord's calls didn't stop. Grocery expenses only seemed to grow. There was no one else to turn to, no backup plan, no safety net. So, Prabhat did what he had to do—he put aside his dreams, put his education on hold, and threw himself into the grind of the BPO industry. It didn't matter that he had no experience. It didn't matter that he was barely out of college. What mattered was that he had a salary, however small, to keep the family afloat.

His days blurred into nights, filled with monotonous chat conversations, troubleshooting software issues for customers who sometimes didn't even know how to turn their computers on. The irony wasn't lost on him—he spent his shifts solving problems for strangers while his own life spiraled into uncertainty. His biggest fear wasn't an angry customer or a failed QA score—it was missing a payment, failing to provide, letting his family down. Every chat closed was just another step closer to paying the next bill, another tick on his performance report, another reason to keep going despite the exhaustion weighing him down.

And then there was Anjali. If Prabhat's struggle was about sudden responsibility, hers was about a lifelong battle. She had grown up knowing what it meant to sacrifice, to put others before herself. The eldest of three siblings, she had taken on the role of second parent long before she was even old enough to understand what that meant.

Her mornings didn't begin with coffee and a relaxed start to the day. Instead, they started before sunrise, in a flurry of responsibilities. She'd wake up early to prepare her siblings for school, making sure they ate before leaving, packing their lunches, reminding them to behave. Then, she would step out to haggle with the vegetable vendor, stretching every rupee, calculating in her head how long the groceries would last. By the time she finally sat at her workstation for her shift, she was already exhausted—physically, emotionally, mentally.

But there was no room for tiredness in the BPO world. The moment her shift started, she became "Agent Anjali"—calm, professional, endlessly patient. “I completely understand your concern,” she would type, even as customers unleashed their frustration over a delayed delivery. What those customers didn’t know was that Anjali, too, was waiting—waiting for relief, waiting for rest, waiting for her sacrifices to finally amount to something.

The weight of responsibility pressed on her from all sides. Her mother, struggling to keep the household together, leaned on her for financial support. Her siblings looked up to her, unknowingly adding to the pressure she carried. And yet, no one at work saw any of this. To them, she was just another agent, another name on a shift roster, another employee hitting targets and closing tickets.

Life for Prabhat and Anjali was a cruel paradox. They were young enough to dream but too burdened to chase those dreams. Every chat they closed, every shift they completed, was another step toward keeping their families afloat. But at what cost? Their youth was slipping away, one chat window at a time, one shift at a time. Their struggles remained invisible to the world—just another agent on the other side of the screen, replying to strangers who would never know their names, let alone the battles they fought every single day.

Days went by, each one blending seamlessly into the next, a repetitive cycle of logins, chats, and exhaustion. The weight of monotony pressed down on me, but there was a light at the end of the tunnel—resignation. First, Vishal left. He walked out of the office with a forced smile, but there was no mistaking the relief in his eyes. It was the look of someone who had finally broken free, who no longer had to wake up dreading another day of mind-numbing work. Then, it was Anshuman’s turn. One by one, we were disappearing, ghosts of the workforce, leaving behind empty chairs and fading memories.

And then, the spotlight turned to me. My time had come. My last day arrived, and with it came the flood of emotions I wasn’t sure how to process. Relief? Yes. Excitement? Maybe. But also a strange sense of detachment, as if I had already left long before my body followed. Every corner of the office, every workstation, every familiar face had once been a part of my daily routine, but today, it all felt distant—like a chapter in a book I had already finished reading.

But unlike the others, I had already decided—I wasn't going to make a spectacle of my last day. No cakes, no farewell speeches, no staged group photos where everyone pretends to be sad while secretly counting down the minutes until they can get back to work. I didn't want the scripted goodbyes or the half-hearted promises of "Let's stay in touch" that we all knew would never be kept.

I watched as others before me had gone through the motions of their farewells—managers giving generic "We'll miss you" speeches, colleagues offering awkward hugs, and someone from HR forcing a smile while asking them to return their ID card and other accessories. It was all so painfully artificial, like a bad sitcom that kept recycling the same plot. I wanted none of it.

So, I decided I would leave the way I had spent most of my time here—quietly, without fuss, slipping away like an unread email lost in an overcrowded inbox. No grand exit, no looking back. Just logging out one last time and stepping into the world beyond those office doors.

As I logged into my system for the last time, I made a conscious effort to avoid eye contact with anyone. No one around me knew it was my final shift, and I saw no reason to announce it. Why invite questions? Why go through the usual cycle of fake concern and forced goodbyes? I wanted no part of that. For them, it was just another ordinary day, another shift filled with endless chat queues and robotic interactions. But for me? This was the final page of an exhausting chapter, and I was more than ready to turn the page.

The usual chaos of the floor buzzed around me—agents glued to their screens, their faces illuminated by the cold glow of their monitors, fingers tapping away at keyboards like they were playing an endless, losing game. The occasional frustrated sighs, the distant hum of conversations where someone was trying to pacify an irate customer, the sharp clang of a coffee cup hastily placed on a desk—it was all painfully familiar. The same sounds, the same routine, the same cycle of burnout disguised as productivity.

I glanced out the window, my eyes trailing over the towering glass buildings that made up the corporate landscape. From the outside, they stood tall, polished, and proud—symbols of opportunity and ambition, glittering under the sunlight, drawing hopeful job seekers like moths to a flame. But step inside, and you'd see the truth. The glamour fades the moment you realize that these walls don't hold success stories—they trap exhaustion, frustration, and unfulfilled dreams. The so-called career growth is nothing more than a series of promotions that come at the cost of your sanity, and the only real reward for hard work is more work.

The workload here isn't just heavy—it's relentless. The chat queues never stop. The expectations never lower. The demand to be faster, more efficient, more available never ends. And management? They'd rather replace you than support you. To them, you're not a person with ambitions, emotions, or limits—you're a metric, a number on a dashboard, a cog in a machine programmed to run until it breaks down. They call it "team spirit," but in reality, it's just a survival game, a never-ending race where only the numbers matter.

It's ironic how these jobs promise stability but leave you feeling like you're constantly walking a tightrope. Miss a KPI (Key Performance Indicator), take a break that's a minute too long, pause for even a second to catch your breath—and suddenly, you're under scrutiny. There's no space for errors, no room for being human. You're expected to be a machine that never tires, never complains, never slows down. And when you finally reach the breaking point and decide to leave, you realize that the only thing you're taking with you is exhaustion.

I didn't even bother to clear my workstation properly. What was the point? My half-empty water bottle, the stress ball I had squeezed through a thousand frustrating shifts, and the jacket I had draped over my chair one too many nights when the air conditioning felt like it was set to "Arctic Survival Mode"—all left behind. A metaphor, perhaps, for the baggage I no longer wanted to carry.

As I sat there, waiting for my final logout, I felt something unexpected—not sadness, not regret, but liberation. For the first time in years, I was making a choice for myself. No more pretending. No more forcing myself to care about things that drained me. No more playing the game I never signed up for.

It was time to go. And I was more than ready.

When the shift ended, I stood up slowly, taking one last look around. The same flickering monitors, the same exhausted faces, the same dull, fluorescent lighting that had cast its artificial glow over countless long, dreary nights. Nothing had changed—but I had. This place had drained me, pushed me to my limits, and now, finally, I was walking away from it.

I adjusted my chair absentmindedly, a habit from years of working here, but this time, I wouldn't be coming back to sit in it. There was no dramatic farewell, no emotional send-off, no one clapping or wishing me well. No one even noticed as I picked up my things—what little I had left—and made my way toward the exit. And that's exactly how I wanted it.

No forced goodbyes. No awkward small talk. Just me, leaving quietly, as if I had never been there at all.

But as I stepped toward the exit, a strange feeling settled in my chest. Not sadness, not nostalgia—just relief. A deep, overwhelming relief that, for the first time in what felt like ages, I could breathe. No more impossible targets looming over me, no more robotic "I understand your concern" messages, no more pretending to care about things that had long since stopped mattering. I was free.

Or at least, I thought I was.

Because life, as always, had other plans.

Just as I reached the corridor near the break room, I noticed someone standing there. Anjali.

Her presence startled me. How did she know? I had been careful—not a single word, not a single hint. Yet, somehow, she had found out.

She stood there, shifting nervously on her feet, her eyes scanning the crowd as if afraid I might slip away before she could reach me. In her hands, she held something—a small, neatly wrapped box that looked like a cake, as if she had prepared it in advance.

I froze for a second, caught between surprise and something else I couldn't quite name. Anjali wasn't just another colleague—she was one of the few people here who actually understood. We had shared the same struggles, the same late-night shifts where exhaustion sat heavy on our shoulders, the same quiet moments where we had spoken about dreams too distant to chase.

And now, here she was, holding out a gift—one final reminder that, even in a place designed to make you feel disposable, some connections still mattered.

I was already feeling overwhelmed. Leaving this job wasn't just a professional decision—it was an emotional rollercoaster. No matter how toxic the environment had become, this was my first job. My first office. My first colleagues. My first taste of the corporate world. And even though it had drained me in ways I couldn't explain, it also held memories—good ones, bad ones, and everything in between.

I had just submitted my ID card and was walking towards the exit when Anjali stopped me. "Wait," she said, her voice firm but soft.

I turned around to see her standing there, a small crowd of my colleagues gathering around her. The cake sat on a table, waiting to be cut. For a moment, I froze. I didn't know whether to laugh, cry, or run away.

Oops, that might have happened if I had announced it. If I had made a big deal out of my departure, maybe there would have been handshakes, forced smiles, or even a half-hearted "Stay in touch." But reality? It was far from that.

No one gave a damn. No farewell messages, no nostalgic recollections of "good old times," no manager stopping me for a last-minute guilt trip. Just silence.

I walked to the reception, handed over my ID card without a word, and watched as they took it without even looking up. No questions, no hesitation—just another employee checked off the list.

I took one last look around, not out of sentimentality, but to confirm what I had always known. This place was never mine, and I was never really a part of it.

And with that, I turned around and walked out. No goodbyes, no fanfare—just freedom.

The next day, which was supposed to be my last working day, my phone buzzed non-stop with missed calls and messages.

Karan. Saloni. Anjali. Their names flashed across my screen, one after the other, each call, each message carrying a piece of the farewell I thought I wouldn't get. Even Aditya, a new joiner who barely knew me beyond a few casual interactions, had sent a message—a simple yet heartfelt wish for good luck, a small acknowledgment that I had existed in this place, even if only for a while.

For a moment, I stared at my screen, feeling an odd warmth spread through me. Maybe I had mattered, after all. Maybe my time here hadn't been as invisible as I thought.

But even as my phone kept lighting up with messages, there was one name missing.

Mohak.

No call. No message. Not even a half-assed "Take care" text.

Mohak—my TL, my so-called friend, the one person I had once thought understood me in this chaotic corporate maze—had chosen silence.

I tried to ignore it, told myself it didn't matter. People drift apart. Friendships fade. Maybe this was just another chapter closing, as it should. But deep down, beneath all the logic and indifference I tried to mask it with, it stung. More than it should have.

Maybe because a part of me had still expected something, even after everything.

The weight of everything I was leaving behind hit me all at once as I walked out of the building. It wasn't just a job I was leaving—it was a part of me. A part that had been shaped, scarred, and tested by this place. And now, as I stepped into the unknown, I carried with me the lessons, the memories, and the bittersweet ache of letting go.

I came here imagining success and financial freedom waiting for me at the end of this journey. But now, as I walk away, all I carry are tears and an empty pocket. It's ironic, really. This place, which I thought would be my ticket to greatness, left me feeling like I had time-traveled backward—like I'd been stripped of not just money but also my confidence and purpose.

It felt as if I'd been stuck in a coma, with my mind completely paralyzed. Days turned into nights, and nights into weeks, but I wasn't living. I was merely surviving, caught in a loop that dulled my senses and drained my energy. Each day here chipped away a little more of who I was, and by the time I realized it, there wasn't much left of the person who had walked in with big dreams and bigger ambitions.

Now, as I step out into the world again, it's not just the weight of failure I carry—it's the heavy silence of lessons learned the hard way. And somewhere deep down, there's a small voice telling me that this, too, will shape me into something stronger. But for now, all I can feel is the ache of what could have been.

These are the questions that linger like unanswered echoes in the minds of those swept up in the whirlwind of the BPO industry. Why do people willingly walk into this world, knowing the trials that await them? Why is the turnover so relentless, with fresh faces greeting the floor one month, only to vanish the next? And why do agents—some of whom possess remarkable potential—end up treated like interchangeable cogs in a machine, enduring relentless mental and emotional strain?

To understand, you have to step back and look at the allure of it all. For many, the BPO sector isn't just an option—it's a lifeline. It offers a quick fix in a world where opportunities are often scarce. The job doesn't demand degrees from elite institutions or specialized skills honed over years. What it does ask for is a voice that can soothe or sell and an adaptability that can bend but never break.

For someone desperate to make ends meet or eager to claim their first taste of independence, a BPO job can feel like salvation. It's a chance to step into a structured world where the paycheck comes on time, and the work—though demanding—offers a semblance of routine. The promise of stability is hard to ignore, even when deep down, they know it's fleeting.

But beneath that promise lies a price no one warns you about. The toll is subtle at first, a gradual erosion of the spirit. The constant pressure to perform, the endless metrics to meet, and the scripted conversations that leave little room for individuality chip away at one's confidence. What starts as a stepping stone often morphs into a trap, ensnaring people in a cycle of stagnation.

It's not just the monotony of the work; it's the weight of being seen as nothing more than a voice on the other end of the line. The emotional exhaustion of placating irate customers or selling something you don't believe in gnaws at your core. And while the first paycheck might sparkle with promise, it rarely accounts for the cost to mental health, relationships, and personal growth.

So, the questions persist—haunting, unanswered. Why do they stay? Or rather, why do they leave? For those caught in the unrelenting grind of the BPO world, the answers aren't simple. They're buried under layers of necessity, ambition, and sometimes, sheer survival.

And the cycle continues because the industry has normalized this treatment. It's a place where employees are often viewed as replaceable, their efforts underappreciated, and their potential stifled by monotonous tasks and overwhelming pressure. Those who endure it over time, from ages 18 to 35, often begin to lose sight of their own aspirations. They get trapped in a system where they're neither growing nor thriving, but merely surviving. And in many cases, the people who stay the longest end up being the ones who have given up on looking for something better, having resigned themselves to the idea that this is all they deserve.

Why isn't anyone regulating this, you ask? The answer is complex. The BPO industry, in many countries, is a major economic force, providing jobs to millions. But the focus is often on numbers—on productivity and meeting targets—rather than on the well-being of the workers who drive the success of these companies. It's a system built to churn out results at the expense of individuals.

So, while employees continue to sign up, hoping for stability, what they often end up losing is their sense of purpose, their motivation, and their well-being. They exchange short-term financial gain for long-term emotional and mental exhaustion, and the cycle repeats itself, as the industry remains focused on profits over people.

Before leaving the city, I asked Anshuman and Vishal where they planned to go next. Their answer was almost predictable, yet it still hit me in a way I wasn't prepared for.

"Another BPO," they both said, almost in unison.

And that's the cruel cycle of this industry. It doesn't just drain you while you're in it—it convinces you that there's nowhere else to go. It cages you in a loop where every exit seems to lead right back to another identical door.

Once you work in a BPO, it slowly eats away at your self-worth, making you believe that this is all you're good for. It dulls your ambitions, makes you question your own potential, and turns survival into the only goal.

First, there's no real reason to pursue further studies or skills development. After all, you're earning well enough to get by. But the truth is, that paycheck is never enough to secure a future or allow for real progress. The focus is always on the present—money coming in, bills getting paid. That's it. It's the perfect trap. The lifestyle seems easy and comfortable for a while, until it isn't.

If you ask anyone working in a BPO, they'll tell you that their salary is barely enough to make ends meet. Many are living on credit cards, trying to stay afloat. The illusion of financial security fades quickly when you realize that you're barely scraping by, with nothing left for growth or saving.

And that's the cycle. People leave one BPO only to find themselves in another, hoping for a fresh start, but nothing really changes. The same soul-crushing work, the same impossible targets, the same feeling of being trapped in a system designed to exhaust you.

The culture of self-doubt and stagnation follows them like a shadow. It's subtle at first—just a lingering thought that maybe they should be doing something more. But over time, it grows, settling into their minds like an unshakable truth: this is all there is.

Breaking free isn't easy. When every new job feels like a recycled version of the last—just a different name on the offer letter, a different office building, but the same suffocating emptiness inside—where do you even begin to look for something more?

They never stop to ask themselves what they truly want. Not because they don't have dreams, but because somewhere along the way, they forgot they were allowed to chase them.

And so, they keep moving—not forward, just around in circles. Going through the motions of life, clutching onto the fleeting hope that something might eventually change.

But deep down, they already know the truth.

They're stuck.

And the worst part? They don't know if they'll ever find a way out.

Last Note

In the Shoes of the Agents

As I sit here, reflecting on the years I spent in the BPO industry, the memories come rushing back in waves. There are days filled with excitement and hope, and there are days when the weight of it all felt unbearable. The BPO industry, a sector that promises to lift people from modest beginnings and propel them into a seemingly prosperous future, has a dual nature. For some, it's a stepping stone to a better life, but for others, it's an unrelenting cycle that drags them deeper into burnout, emotional exhaustion, and disillusionment. I've walked both paths, and as I close this chapter of my life, I'm left to untangle the complexity of it all: the good, the bad, and everything in between.

The Bright Beginnings: The Allure of the BPO World

When I first stepped into the world of BPO, it was like entering a new realm—a world of opportunity, financial stability, and hope. The entry requirement was simple: a basic education and a willingness to work hard. For someone like me, who didn't have a clear academic path ahead, the BPO industry seemed like a perfect solution. It promised a steady paycheck, an opportunity to live independently, and even the possibility of quick advancement.

What struck me the most during my early days was the camaraderie. You weren't just working with colleagues; you were working with friends—people who shared the same struggles, who understood the same pressures, and who laughed through the long shifts together. The team spirit was strong, and we were all driven by the same goal: to keep the clients happy, meet our targets, and go home to get some sleep before the next shift began.

And the pay wasn't bad either. Compared to other entry-level jobs, the salary was decent, and the bonuses for performance gave us an added incentive to push harder. Many of us who joined right out of school were living comfortably, and for the first time, I felt financially independent. The possibility of incentives for exceeding targets made me feel like I could rise above my circumstances. And the best part was, the BPO industry didn't require me to be a graduate with a specific degree. It offered me the chance to build something for myself.

The training programs were another upside. They didn't just teach us how to handle customer calls; they taught us life skills. How to communicate effectively, how to stay calm under pressure, how to solve problems on the spot—skills that, in hindsight, are incredibly valuable in any job. The exposure to an international clientele was also an eye-opener. The BPO industry opened the doors to a global economy, teaching me to navigate different cultures and understand how business is done across borders. It was exciting.

The Reality: The Darker Side of BPO Life

But as time passed, the shine began to wear off. The BPO world, which had promised growth and stability, started showing its darker side. The reality of working in this environment isn't as glamorous as it first seemed.

First came the pressure. The constant targets, the daily performance metrics, and the ever-watchful eyes of supervisors. Every chats, every customer interaction, was scrutinized for perfection. A single slip-up could result in a scolding, a warning, or worse, a deduction in pay. The sense of accomplishment I initially felt began to erode as I realized that no matter how much I gave, it was never enough. I was expected to do more, to perform better, to push harder—every single day.

The worst part wasn't the pressure to meet targets, though. It was the mental and emotional toll of constantly being in the firing line. The customers were often upset, angry, or frustrated, and no matter how calm or polite you were, it didn't matter. If you failed to resolve their issue within the set time, they'd disconnected on you, leaving you feeling like a failure. The emotional exhaustion was draining.

And then there were the long hours. The night shifts were particularly grueling, disrupting your sleep schedule and affecting your physical health. Sitting at a desk for eight or more hours a day, with barely any time to stretch your legs, led to back pain, poor posture, and fatigue. The body aches became a part of the routine, but I pushed through, convinced that it was all for a bigger goal.

But what really started to eat away at me was the constant fear of being replaced. In the BPO world, you're expendable. If you're not performing, if you're not meeting targets, if you're not following the script, there's always someone else ready to take your place. The turnover rate is high, and every new hire is trained with the same hope of doing better, only to fall into the same cycle of burnout.

The Spiral of Self-Doubt: How BPO Changes You

As the months dragged on, I started to notice something unsettling—the version of myself that had walked into this industry full of hope and ambition was slowly fading away. The eager, optimistic person who had once believed in career growth, new opportunities, and a future beyond customer support was now just a distant memory. In his place stood someone I barely recognized.

The change wasn't sudden; it crept in quietly, day by day, shift by shift. At first, it was just minor things—I stopped talking about where I saw myself in five years, brushed off thoughts about pursuing something bigger, and started convincing myself that maybe this was enough. But soon, that doubt took deeper roots. My dreams, which once felt possible, now seemed naïve. I told myself I was being "realistic," but the truth was, I was settling.

I wasn't the only one. I watched it happen to my colleagues, too—people who had once been so full of life, so eager to prove themselves. I had seen them walk in on their first day with bright eyes and high hopes, talking about how this was just a stepping stone, a temporary stop on their way to something greater. But months turned into years, and those dreams started to crumble.

The BPO industry doesn't just drain your energy—it slowly chips away at your self-worth. It convinces you that this is the best you can do, that there's nothing better out there for you. And once that thought settles in, escaping becomes harder than ever.

The atmosphere in the office changed, too. What was once a lively, buzzing workplace filled with jokes and camaraderie had turned into something far more toxic. The casual banter during breaks had been replaced by whispered conversations about stress, anxiety, and survival strategies. No one laughed as much anymore. Instead of discussing weekend plans, people were talking about their growing exhaustion, their frustrations with management, and their fears of being laid off. Hope was no longer the dominant emotion—fear was.

What disturbed me the most was how the conversation around the future had shifted. No one spoke about long-term goals or ambitions anymore. Nobody said, "I want to move up the ladder," or "I plan to switch careers soon." Instead, all I heard was:

"I just need to get through this month."

"Let me just survive this shift."

"If I can hold on until the next paycheck, I'll figure things out."

It was heartbreaking. People weren't thinking ahead anymore; they were just trying to make it through the day. The idea of personal growth, of learning new skills, of actually building a career—it all felt like a distant dream, something only lucky people got to do.

And at some point, I realized I had started thinking the same way.

The Financial Strain: A Cycle of Debt and Despair

For all the talk of decent salaries in the BPO industry, the reality was far from it. The paychecks were enough to get by, but they were never enough to build a stable financial future. The cost of living—rent, utilities, transportation, and basic necessities—consumed nearly every penny we earned. The concept of saving money or making meaningful investments seemed like a distant dream, something reserved for those with significantly higher incomes or lower daily expenses.

Many of us found ourselves stuck in an endless cycle of living paycheck to paycheck. Each month, we would receive our salaries, pay off bills, cover necessary expenses, and be left with little to nothing. The struggle was real, and for many, it became increasingly difficult to maintain financial stability. To bridge the gap, many agents resorted to credit cards, personal loans, and borrowing money from friends or family, just to make it through the month. These temporary fixes, however, came with their own set of problems, pushing us deeper into debt with high interest rates, late payment fees, and the constant stress of repayment.

The financial security promised when we first entered the industry felt like an illusion. We had believed that our hard work would be rewarded with stability, but the reality was far from it. The long hours, the emotional toll of dealing with irate customers, the physical exhaustion from night shifts—all of it drained us. Rather than being able to focus on financial growth or future planning, we were left scrambling just to meet immediate obligations.

The demands of the job left little room for pursuing other income sources or skill development that could lead to better opportunities. Many of us were too exhausted to take on side hustles or enroll in courses that could open doors to higher-paying roles. Instead, we remained trapped in the cycle—work hard, earn just enough to survive, and then spend it all just to make it through another month. The system seemed designed to keep us in this state, ensuring that we remained dependent on our salaries without ever truly advancing.

For the majority, this was not just a temporary struggle but a long-term reality. The cycle of debt became a defining aspect of the BPO lifestyle, one that was nearly impossible to break free from. Even for those who managed to earn slightly more over time, the increasing cost of living always seemed to catch up, preventing any real progress. The dream of financial independence remained out of reach for many, replaced instead by the daily grind of working just to survive.

Breaking free from this cycle required more than just financial discipline—it demanded a shift in industry standards, better wages, and opportunities for true financial growth. Until then, for countless BPO workers, the reality remained the same: work tirelessly, earn enough to get by, and repeat the cycle endlessly, with no real escape in sight.

The Government's Role: A Call for Change

The government plays a pivotal role in shaping industries that contribute significantly to the economy, and the Business Process Outsourcing (BPO) sector is no exception. As one of the largest sources of employment and revenue generation, the BPO industry has helped boost economic growth and provided job opportunities for thousands. However, while the industry thrives, its workforce often faces harsh working conditions that demand immediate attention. The government must step in to ensure the welfare of BPO employees by addressing key issues such as excessive working hours, inadequate wages, insufficient benefits, and the lack of mental health support. One of the most pressing concerns in the BPO industry is the long and often erratic working hours, particularly for those who work night shifts to cater to international clients. These extended hours can lead to chronic fatigue, sleep disorders, and overall health deterioration. Without adequate rest and regulated working conditions, employees may experience burnout, ultimately affecting their productivity and well-being. To counter this, the government should introduce legislation that strictly enforces regulated working hours, ensuring that no employee is overworked without sufficient rest periods. Policies mandating regular breaks, proper scheduling to avoid excessive overtime, and regular health assessments should be implemented. These regulations would not only improve the quality of life for BPO employees but also enhance their efficiency and job satisfaction, ultimately benefiting the industry as a whole. Although the BPO industry is known for offering competitive salaries for entry-level positions, the reality is that wages often fail to match the rising cost of living. Many BPO workers struggle to make ends meet, particularly when factoring in expenses such as housing, transportation, healthcare, and family support. The government must take proactive measures to ensure that BPO workers receive fair compensation that aligns with the economic demands of modern life. This includes setting a standardized living wage that allows employees to afford essential needs, save for the future, and enjoy a balanced lifestyle. Additionally, there should be policies that guarantee essential benefits such as healthcare coverage, paid sick leave, retirement plans, and opportunities for career growth. These changes will not only uplift workers but also encourage talent retention in the industry, reducing turnover rates and improving overall job satisfaction. Working in the BPO industry can be mentally and emotionally taxing. Employees frequently deal with irate customers, challenging work environments, and the pressures of meeting performance targets. The cumulative stress from these factors often leads to anxiety, depression, and even long-term psychological issues. Despite these challenges, mental health support remains severely lacking within the industry. The government must recognize mental health as a critical aspect of worker welfare and implement programs to provide accessible mental health resources. This includes offering free or subsidized counseling services, therapy sessions, and stress management workshops. Additionally, companies should be encouraged to create a supportive work culture that prioritizes employee well-being, incorporating initiatives such as wellness programs, peer support groups, and mental health days. The BPO industry plays an essential role in the economy, but its success should not come at the expense of its workers. The government must step up and take responsibility by implementing policies that regulate working hours, ensure fair wages, and provide adequate mental health support. By doing so, not only will the lives of BPO employees improve, but the industry will also thrive with a healthier, more motivated workforce. Now is the time for action—workers deserve better, and the government has the power to bring about meaningful change.

The Final Decision: A Life Beyond the BPO

As I reflect on my time in the BPO industry, I realize that it has shaped me in ways I could never have predicted. The fast-paced environment, the high-pressure targets, and the ever-changing dynamics of customer service have all left an indelible mark on me. The skills I learned—communication, adaptability, problem-solving, and resilience—are assets that I will carry forward in my journey. The friendships I made, forged in the trenches of demanding shifts and shared struggles, have become some of the most meaningful connections in my life. And the lessons—both personal and professional—will stay with me forever.

However, I have also come to understand that the BPO industry is not for everyone. For some, it is a stepping stone—a means to an end, a way to earn a living, to support a family, or to fund dreams that lie beyond the confines of a headset and a cubicle. For others, it becomes a long-term career, offering stability, growth, and the opportunity to climb the corporate ladder. But for many, it is a relentless cycle that drains them emotionally, mentally, and even physically. The demanding hours, the unpredictability of the job, and the toll it takes on one's well-being can sometimes make it a soul-crushing experience.

As I stand at this crossroads, leaving the BPO world behind, I find myself faced with a crucial choice. What comes next? Will I take the familiar route and continue in the industry, accepting its pros and cons as a necessary trade-off? Or will I break free and pursue something that truly ignites my passion and gives me a sense of purpose and fulfillment?

The choice is yours, too. Whether you are currently in the BPO industry, contemplating joining, or thinking of leaving, take a moment to reflect on your own path. What do you truly want from life? What are you willing to endure, and what are you willing to fight for? These are questions only you can answer. It's easy to stay where it's comfortable, to follow a path that is predictable. But true growth often requires stepping into the unknown, embracing uncertainty, and trusting yourself to navigate whatever comes next.

For me, the decision was clear. While the BPO life had its moments of reward and camaraderie, the downsides became too steep a price to pay. I chose to walk away—not just from the job but from the toxic cycle it had created in my life. The sleepless nights, the stress-induced fatigue, the sense of being trapped in a never-ending loop—it was time to reclaim my peace, my happiness, and my sanity.

Walking away was not easy. There was fear, self-doubt, and the daunting question of "What now?" But I knew that staying in an environment that drained me was not an option. I had to take a leap of faith, to trust that there was more waiting for me beyond the confines of this industry.

And so, I chose to pursue something that aligns with my true aspirations. Whether that means further education, a new career path, or an entrepreneurial venture, I am embracing the unknown with an open heart and an open mind. Life is too short to settle for something that does not fulfill you. If you find yourself in a similar place, know that you are not alone. Your happiness and well-being are worth fighting for. Sometimes, the hardest decisions lead to the most rewarding destinations.

The BPO industry gave me experience, friendships, and valuable lessons—but now, it is time for a new chapter. And for those who feel stuck, remember: you have the power to change your story too.

www.ingramcontent.com/pod-product-compliance
Lightning Source LLC
LaVergne TN
LVHW041102150826
845673LV00007B/1882

* 9 7 9 8 8 9 7 4 4 2 2 7 0 *